D0522929

The Name
of a Bullfighter

THE AUTHOR

Luis Sepúlveda was born in 1949 in Chile. He was exiled for his political activities in 1975 and worked in the Amazonian jungle for UNESCO. Since 1980 he has lived in Germany.

The Name
of a Bullfighter

Luis Sepúlveda

Translated from the Spanish
by Suzanne Ruta

a&b

This edition published in Great Britain in 1997 by
Allison & Busby Ltd
114 New Cavendish Street
London W1M 7FD

A catalogue record for this book is available from the
British Library

ISBN 0 74900 355 3

Printed and bound in Great Britain by
WBC Book Manufacturers Ltd
Bridgend, Mid Glamorgan

08575632

TO MY NOBLE FRIENDS:

Ricardo Bada
(who convinced me I was a writer)

Paco Ignacio Taibo
(who introduced me to the possibilities of the roman noir*)*

and Jaime Casas, aka Porky
(who lived a dark roman noir *but never failed
to brighten his surroundings)*

Part One

*Sooner or later life is going to cross my path
and I'll spring into action. Like a lion.*

HAROLDO CONTI,
Argentine writer disappeared in Buenos Aires,
May 4, 1976

CHAPTER ONE

Tierra del Fuego:
Chimangos in the Sky

The bus was called *Star of the Pampas.* The driver's eyes lit
up when he saw the form of a horseman by the side of
the road. For five hours he'd been staring at a straight
stretch of highway, with nothing to break the monotony
but a pair of rheas he scared off by banging on the horn.
Before him lay the road, to his left the broom grass and
barberry bushes of the pampas, to his right the sea, flowing
through the Strait of Magellan with an incessant hateful
rippling. And that was it.

The horseman was about two hundred yards up ahead.
He was sitting on a shaggy old nag, which grazed calmly.
The horseman's body was encased in a black poncho that
covered the flanks of his mount as well. His narrow-
brimmed gaucho hat had slid down over his eyes. Not a
muscle on him twitched. The driver stopped the bus and
elbowed his assistant.

"Wake up, Pacheco!"

"Huh? I wasn't sleeping, boss."

"No? Your snoring drowned out the motor. Some help you are."

"I'm sorry. It's this road. The same damn thing all the time. Want a maté?"

"Look. The old jerk is nodding off, or fast asleep."

"There's only one way to find out, boss."

There were only a handful of passengers on the bus, and they were stiff and sore after many hours on the road. Some were dozing, heads bent forward. The others chatted halfheartedly about soccer upsets, or the steadily falling price of wool. The driver turned toward them, pointed to the still figure of the man on horseback, and signaled for them to be quiet.

The *Star of the Pampas* rolled slowly forward and came to a stop alongside the sleeping horseman. The horse didn't flinch, but went on nibbling at the sparse grass. Horse and rider were parked next to a strange wooden building, painted red and yellow. It was a sort of birdhouse on stilts, raised five feet off the ground, and large enough for a man to sleep comfortably inside.

The harsh blare of the horn startled the horse. He stretched his neck, shook his head, eyes wide with fear, and backed away, nearly dislodging the rider.

"Whoa, whoa, dumbbell," the befuddled rider shouted.

"Wake up, you old jerk. I nearly ran over you," the

bus driver greeted him, while his assistant and the passengers roared with laughter.

"Villain! Rascal! Wretch!" the rider replied, striking the horse's neck to make it hold still.

"Don't lose your temper; you could have a stroke. And get out of the way; we have to load the mail into the box."

"Do you have anything for me, you lout?"

"How should I know? The regulations say you have to look in the box for your mail."

The assistant stepped off the bus. He went over to the odd-looking structure and opened the door marked POST BOX 5. TIERRA DEL FUEGO. He reached in and removed several cartons, bundles of hides, and a sack with the emblem of the Chilean Postal Service. He took all this into the bus and returned a few minutes later carrying a load of battered packages and another mailbag. He stowed them inside and gave the door a resounding slam.

"All right, let's see if anyone remembered you."

The horseman waited for the *Star of the Pampas* to move off. He watched the bus recede in the distance till it was only a flickering afterimage in the uniform panorama of the pampas. Then he spurred his horse and went over to the mailbox.

The letter read as follows: "I'm sorry, Hans. They're coming for you, the same ones as always. See you in hell. Your friend, Ulrich."

"Good. It had to happen sometime. I've been waiting

for more than forty years. They can come when they're ready," he muttered, rereading the letter while the wind whipped at it.

His silver spurs touched the horse's flanks lightly and set it trotting away from the road and through the plain of tall shiny broom grass glinting in the midday sun. Suddenly he tugged at the reins and pulled his horse up short. He stood in the stirrups and gazed into the sky. High overhead hovered a pair of chimangos, ugly carrion hawks.

"How is it those big birds are always the first to smell trouble?" he asked out loud. Then he dug in his spurs and galloped away.

Berlin: Auf Wiedersehen
(Adiós, Pampa Mia)

I know this letter will be quite disjointed, but you must be aware that memory is not always infallible, and you can't make a tidy confession when you have a betrayal weighing on your conscience.

I betrayed a man. That man was my best friend. But feelings have no place in this nasty business, so I'll just lay out the facts.

In 1941 Hans Hillermann and I were serving in the police of the Third Reich. We were not Nazis. We made no notable contribution to the persecution of the Jews or the repression of dissidents. Our assignment in Berlin was to guard the main gate of Spandau prison.

Winters in Berlin were harsh. They still are. At that time, the prison authorities had set aside a small heated room in the basement of the building where we guards could thaw out and drink a cup of coffee now and then. Hans and I were old friends, the bond between us strengthened by interminable chess games and our secret desire to clear out for good, to emigrate someday, to a place we'd heard was the last promising spot on the planet: Tierra del Fuego. We gathered information on this faraway frontier from travelers' chronicles and geography books. They fueled our imaginations and our longing to leave Germany. I was born in Saxony, Hans in Hamburg. He knew everyone in the harbor district, and was always saying how easy it would be to ship out. We had our plan ready, we were actually going to desert. What we didn't have was money. And so we spent long nights in the heated prison basement, moving chess pieces across the board and bemoaning the poverty that condemned us to a life in uniform.

At one point, I no longer remember just when, finding ourselves alone, we grew daring and forced the lock on a door that led to a sort of storeroom. We knew that SS officials used that side room. We'd seen them coming in and out with carefully wrapped packages. We forced the lock, in hopes of finding a good bottle of wine or brandy to liven up guard duty, but all we saw were flat, lightweight packages. We opened one, very carefully. It was a painting. Neither Hans nor I knew anything about art, but we reasoned that if the SS were keeping these paintings, they had to be valuable. I remember Hans saying, "Well, Ulrich, it looks as if we're getting closer to our journey."

We frequently attacked that door and gave ourselves up to the contemplation of various works of art. Often too, we felt tempted to take one for ourselves and desert. What stopped us was the bitter realization that we didn't know what to do with the painting. How could we determine its value? To whom could we sell it? Besides, as soon as the SS noticed it was missing, they would have no trouble catching up with the thieves. We had a notion of the enormous wealth within our reach, and our ignorance was a torment to us. Several months went by in this manner, till one night, on guard duty, we forced that lock again. This time we found a sturdy wooden crate. We opened it, taking care not to bend the nails or dent the boards. Inside, beneath layers of wrapping, was a smaller box, shut with a heavy bronze lock. On the face of the lock we read the words "Hanseatic Lloyd's, Hamburg."

The sight of that lock tempted us powerfully. We jimmied it, well aware we were taking the biggest risk of our lives. What we discovered in that box took our breath away. Sixty-three gold coins.

We hugged each other for joy. At last the dream we had shared for so long was about to come true. Hans was the first to get over his excitement. He returned the coins to the box and said, "Ulrich, we'd better get going right now. These coins are worth more than we can imagine. Let's go now, and decide what to do with the coins later. They'll be looking for us high and low, so the farther away we get, the better."

We arrived in Hamburg in November 1941. Hans really did have connections among the dockworkers. While we were waiting for our getaway ship, he confided in me as never before. I learned, for example, that he was a militant Spartacist, and that a brother of his had died in Spain, fighting alongside other international volunteers in the Thälmann Brigade.

Dockworkers who were Spartacists hid us in a house in Altona.

There we spent three weeks, waiting for the ship recommended to us. We were to travel in the hold of the Lebu, *a Chilean steamship that anchored in Hamburg twice a year with a cargo of lumber. While we were waiting, I remember asking him if he had any idea as to how* we would sell the coins. His reply was not exactly reassuring, "Forget it, Ulrich. We'll never sell them. We have to wait till the war is over to deal with them. Then we'll see whether their owners try to reclaim them, or if we melt them down. I'm afraid it will be a long time till we can cash in."

One night the brown beast caught up with us.

I don't know if someone informed on us, or if the house where we were staying had been targeted by the Gestapo from the start. Hans nevertheless managed to flee. He took the coins with him.

I don't suppose there's any need to give details of what I suffered at the hands of the Gestapo. When I lost track of the weeks, or was it months, they'd been holding me, I decided Hans must be safe, and in the confessions I signed now and then I never admitted to anything beyond my own complicity in the theft. I knew from my slight experience as a policeman that these men would not kill before they had obtained the information they needed: my partner's whereabouts.

They knew their stuff. The beatings and torture were steady and systematic, but never put my life or my sanity at risk. They knew that a madman would slip through their fingers for good. I held out for four years, clinging to the three words that never crossed my lips, although they were indelibly tatooed on my brain: Tierra del Fuego.

In June 1945 some Russian soldiers found me in the basement of Gestapo headquarters. I couldn't walk. A spinal injury left my legs out of commission for good. They extricated me from there. I saw the light of day. I saw Berlin in ruins. I learned that Germany had surrendered, that the Third Reich no longer existed, that the nightmare was ending.

I invented a tale for the benefit of the Russian intelligence officers who interrogated me. I told them I'd been a policeman, arrested by the Gestapo as a militant antifascist. To enhance the credibility of my story, I gave them the names of the Spartacists who helped us in Hamburg. As luck would have it, all these men had died during the war. Since there were no witnesses to refute my version of events, it was accepted.

Early in 1946, the Russians transferred me to Moscow for medical treatment. There was nothing to be done for my legs, and so, after I'd spent five years in a wheelchair, identifying the Nazis among thousands of German soldiers held as prisoners of war, I was permitted to return to Berlin. My plan was to leave Germany and travel to Tierra del Fuego, one way or another. I was fully confident that Hans had managed to reach his destination and was waiting for me with my share of the booty. But when you're disabled your thoughts move more quickly than you do. I found I had become a citizen of the German Democratic Republic, locked up in an open prison that claimed to be the socialist paradise.

I heard from Hans for the first time in 1955. I don't know how he managed to send a letter from Sydney. Perhaps some traveler agreed to take it. The message was terse, but said it all. "I hear you have health problems. You know where I am. It's a good place to mend one's bones."

That terse letter annoyed the Stasi no end. The nightmare began all over again. Threats. Beatings. More threats. More beatings. They had the story of the coins down pat. They wanted to know where in Australia Hans was living. They sat me down in front of a map of Australia, hundreds of times. And every time, I spun them a tale. It's a good thing Australia is a continent. In short, for as long as the GDR lasted, I was totally prohibited from leaving Berlin. Every letter I received was first read and analyzed by the Stasi, and the file with my name on it contained over a thousand pages.

For fifty years I kept the secret of Hans's whereabouts, and the location of the coins. For fifty years I dreamed of our reunion, and a chance to enjoy that booty. When the GDR collapsed like a house of cards, I thought at last the moment I'd been longing for had come. I had some savings, enough to book a flight to South America; my passport was in order. There was no one and nothing to keep me from traveling. Or so I thought until a few days ago, when I fell into the hands of a pair of armed perps, former Nazis who later became Communists, and I'll be damned if I know what they are now.

They held me up right in downtown Berlin, two men I already knew. Former Stasi agents.

"Let's go. We have to talk about Hans Hillermann," they said. They hoisted me out of my wheelchair and shoved me into a car. They worked so fast there was no time to holler for help then, or later either, because they took me out of the car in an underground parking garage and carried me upstairs on a stretcher, to an office with the name of a real estate agency on the door. But glancing out the window, I could see we were on the Kurfürstendamm.

For the first time, my interrogation was conducted by a man they call the Major. He showed me the voluminous file with my name on it. Fanning himself with the pages, he gave me to understand that if they hadn't taken drastic action with me before this, it was because they were waiting patiently for me to make the big mistake.

The mistake was not of my making. Hans had written a second

letter, as brief as the earlier one. The Major had it on his desk. "Nothing to keep you from coming now. Inform when arriving you know where. Post Box Number 5." The letter was postmarked Santiago, Chile.

A man can endure a great deal of pain. The astounding mechanism of the brain provides corners, empty stretches, where you can hide, and there's always the final option of succumbing to madness. To achieve either of these alternatives, you have to believe in "something." You have to see, to feel, that your stubborn silence is keeping this "something" out of the torturers' reach.

When I saw that the letter came from Chile, I realized I had nothing more to believe in. I have always considered myself an atypical German, because I know how to lose.

I couldn't deny to the Major and his men that Hans was in Chile. And no matter what part of the country I mentioned as his place of residence, they would study the whole list of post box number fives, until, by a process of elimination, they found the right one.

And so I betrayed my friend. I betrayed him, but when the Major insisted on knowing the name of the man who had ordered us to commit the robbery, I realized I could still stall him, and make his victory more laborious. If he assumed someone had ordered us to steal the coins, it was because he feared that person might get to them before he did, and suddenly my memory dredged up the words engraved on the lock, Hanseatic Lloyd's, as my trump card.

To gain time, I played along with him. I dropped the name of the man who was chief of police in Berlin in 1941. The Major consulted his computer, and apparently it furnished some interesting data, because suddenly he was beside himself with joy.

I don't know, nor do I care, what shady deals my former boss was involved in. Whatever it was, he helped me to get away. Obviously I wasn't planning to flee. In a wheelchair? But I wanted to get away before the Major realized he had overlooked one important question: my friend's current identity.

They took me down to the underground parking garage. We got back into the car, this time the Major joined us, and we drove out into the streets of Berlin. "You are going to identify your old boss. That's all. You tell us who he is and your part in this business is over," the Major said.

I couldn't even remember what the man looked like. I only saw him a couple of times during the war. But I agreed. They parked the car near the Zoo Station, one of the former Stasi agents started pushing the wheelchair. I waited till we were in the thick of the crowd on the sidewalk. Then I fell to the ground, screaming in pain.

People came running at once, out of curiosity or a desire to help.

"It's my heart. I've had a heart attack before," I said. An ambulance came and took me away. The Major and his men were powerless to prevent it.

There's always something out of whack in a man of seventy-two, especially if he's disabled to begin with.

I am writing to you from the Charlottenburg Hospital. You will find Hans Hillermann and those damned gold coins in Tierra del Fuego. The only address I can provide is as mentioned above. Post Box Number 5. May it be my fortune that this letter reaches you and you catch up with Hans before the Major's men do. My friend now goes by the name of Franz Stahl.

I shall not come out of here alive. I could have told my story to *the police and asked for protection, but this game has lasted so long it would be ludicrous to give it such a silly ending. I am sure Hans will want to play the game to the bitter end. I have written him, simply saying "Sorry, Hans. They're coming for you, the same ones as always. See you in hell."*

By the time you read this letter I'll be on a long journey. I played the game and lost. I lost every time. I'm not angry, or troubled. Losing is just a question of method.

Ulrich Helm
Berlin, February 1991

CHAPTER THREE

Hamburg: Happy Birthday!

The cold woke me that February night. I jumped out of bed. My breath formed a stream of vapor clouds. The first thing I did was check to see if the windows were shut. They were. Then I checked the thermostat. It was on the highest setting, but the radiator was as cold as the floor. I was about to phone the janitor when I heard someone knocking at the door.

I opened. A little man in a blue ski cap pulled down over his eyebrows started giving me explanations in a mixture of German, English, and sign language, showing me a bunch of tools.

"Sorry, I don't understand a word," I said.

"No, the heat, you understand?"

I let him in. He went to the radiator, crouched down, loosened a bolt. Oily water started dripping out. He readjusted the bolt, felt the radiator all over, shook his head, took his walkie-talkie and spoke in classic Chilean:

"We bungled it, dope. I told you so. Over. What? You want me going to every apartment to explain. They don't understand me, asshole. Over."

Shorty held the receiver to his ear a while longer, but evidently his partner had hung up.

"You a Chilean?" I asked.

Shorty nodded yes. He was still waiting for an answer from his comrade.

"What's going on with the heat? It's winter out there."

"It looks like the main pipes are clogged. Trouble is we don't know where. We're going to have to take apart the radiators in every apartment. It's one royal mess, boss."

"Then you can start here. I have to go out in a little while."

"It's not that easy. We have to wait for the contractor. It could take a long time."

"And what are we supposed to do meanwhile? You can't leave me without heat."

"Don't you worry. You leave us your key, but first you sign this form, giving us permission to enter your apartment. I have it right here."

Shorty gave me the form. I filled it out, acceding to the German obsession for biographical data. I signed it and gave it back to him, along with a spare key to the apartment.

"Right. Now I'm going to tell the other tenants. And don't worry, when you get back your heat will be on," he said on his way out.

"I hope so. I'm not cut out to be a penguin."

In the bathroom, I discovered there was no hot water either. I was resigning myself to a dry shave when I heard more knocking at the door. I opened. It was Shorty again. He had the form I filled out in one hand and he was grinning from ear to ear.

"Happy birthday!"

"What? I don't follow."

"It's your birthday. Look, you put down your date of birth here. You see? Happy Birthday!"

Forty-four. Double whammy. Damn that midget for reminding me. Sitting on the toilet I decided there was no point brooding over it. Forty-four. In someone like me, the only distinction about reaching that age, was just that: you had reached that age. Happy birthday. I lit up the day's first smoke and looked at the books piled on the windowsill. That's where I kept the works of Paco Taibo, Jürgen Alberts, Daniel Chavarría. I liked to read them while taking a crap, savoring the undeniable sweetness of revenge in small doses. In their books the characters I identified with, guys on my side, always lost out, but they always knew exactly why, as if their main ambition in life was to formulate an esthetic for that most contemporary of arts: the art of losing gracefully.

The cold drove me out of the apartment. While double locking the door, I felt a stabbing pain in my lower back. I wondered if it was my body suddenly realizing I was forty-four. I headed downstairs. On the second-floor landing I ran into a neighbor couple on their way up with their shopping. Strange people, these neighbors, with their tendency to Ottomanize everything. The guy had a habit of sending letters to the janitor. No matter what I did, he wrote complaining about my annoying Turkish habits. If I was listening to tangos with the volume down low, he bitched about my noisy Muslim liturgies; if I put on a salsa record, he targeted the doubtful morals of a Turk living without a wife in the picture. I said good evening to them. I couldn't care less if they replied. The guy answered me with a grunt, which proved he wasn't deaf, but his wife didn't respond at all, since she was busy shouting at her kids to get the hell upstairs. On my way down I ran into the children, who eyed me suspiciously.

"What's up, dwarves?"

"We're not dwarves and you're a bum," one of them replied.

"And how do you know that?"

"Because our parents told us we'd better study hard so we don't turn out like you, a Turkish bum who gets up at five in the afternoon," the other one explained.

"Sing me a song. Today is my birthday."

"Foreigners don't have birthdays," the first one told

me, and that's as far as he got, before his mother's loving voice was heard from upstairs, threatening to give him a good thrashing.

Night. In the street, the February cold forced people to walk hunched over, as if they were searching for something on the ground. I turned up my coat collar, shoved my hands into my pockets, and walked on. We wouldn't see daylight till the end of March, but that was no cause for complaint. Once summer came and daylight lasted forever, I would long for the nocturnal darkness that makes all cats the same safe shade of gray.

As every evening, a fair-sized river of urine flowed down the stairs of the subway. Avoiding the puddles, I approached the ticket machines. As always, one out of five was working and, as always, next to the machines a small band of joyous drunks was trying to empty a pack of beers in record time. I slid my fare money into the slot.

"Hey. Since when do they let filthy pigs ride the subway?" one of them spat out.

"Beat it back to Anatolia, Mustafa," another grunted.

Here it was nearly six in the evening, yet it seemed to me my day was off to a good start. No heat, insulted by a pair of dwarves, and now these kids stinking of piss. One of the advantages of living in Hamburg is that you get a lot of opportunities for physical exercise. A Nazi is sort of like a talking punching bag, just begging to be slapped, although a number of cowardly intellectuals disguised as pacifists have tried to convince me that this bunch of drunks, say, should not be considered Nazis, but alienated victims of the system, denied access to consumer society. As if Nazism weren't pure unadulterated shit.

"You going or not, you dirty wog?" another inquired.

Yes, indeed barely six in the evening, and my day was off to a good start. Happy Birthday, I said to myself, and let fly with my left foot at the carton of beer cans.

The boys retreated to a prudent distance and continued to insult me from there, while I trampled on their beer cans. Happy Birthday, I scanned, in time to the last moves in my demolition derby. Then I headed for the platform, my shoes filled with foam.

The subway car was full of silent passengers. Some looked me over, with the usual obvious disapproval, and then went back to learning the alphabet from *Bild* magazine. Traveling companions on my brief daily trip, five stops long. A different bunch every night, probably, but to me they all looked alike. Tired out after working an eight-hour day in factories and offices, without the energy or the desire to sit down in a warm café and decide how to spend their hard-earned hours of sweet leisure.

Shut up in themselves, guzzling the inevitable can of lukewarm beer, they headed home to their silent apartments, their silent bread and pickles and sad sliced liverwurst, their uncomfortable slippers, to protect the carpet. They'd have a beer and then another, and then one more, sitting in front of the TV with the volume way down, so they could hear if the neighbor upstairs respected the noise-control law.

A passenger went over to an ad for the Labor Exchange. He read it, took a pencil from his pocket, and made notes on the back of a magazine. I looked at the ad too. It extolled the benefits of job training. "It's never too late to learn."

What could a guy like me learn at the age of forty-four?

I had a job and I had to hold on to it, since, unless I wanted to unload frozen bananas at the docks, my prospects for finding something else were not exactly rosy. What kind of work was a guy like me suited for? Hell, a forty-four-year-old ex-guerrilla. The Hamburg Labor Exchange would not look kindly on my application for job training if, under the heading "What can you do?" I put down: intelligence, counterintelligence, sabotage and related fields, forgery of documents, manufacture of home-made explosives, doctorate in defeat.

I had a job that let me sleep all morning. When I woke up, I spent a couple of hours reading mystery novels, sitting in the bathtub or on the can. At night I served as discreet in-house security guard at the Regina, one of the last remaining cabarets on Grosse Freiheit, Great Freedom Street.

The work was by no means taxing, nor did it require

complex analyses. Old men would get excited by a pair of tits and try to climb on stage to see if those marvels were silicon or real female flesh. It was up to me to make the old boys behave. And it was up to me to explain to the argumentative types in the private booths that our deep-throated girls didn't give discounts. Now and then a cheap-skate would try to appropriate a striptease artist's panties without paying for them, and I'd have to stick my fist in his face. Being a goon in a brothel wasn't bad. I decided I could afford to ignore the suggestions of the Labor Exchange.

When I got out of the subway it was bone-chilling cold. The evening's first whores, bundled up like astro-nauts, were pacing their square yard of sidewalk across from the Davidstrasse police headquarters. Rubbing my hands, I walked to Zelma's Imbiss. The minute I opened the door of the snack bar, the prevailing warmth and the aroma of roasting, dripping souvlaki put me in the mood to celebrate my birthday. Zelma, fat as a barrel, was wrap-ping up two orders of stuffed peppers for a girl.

"How you doing, countryman?" she greeted me.

"Hungry, countrywoman, very hungry."

"And cold, countryman. You're shivering. Go ahead, have a glass of tea."

The girl's order was ready. As she was paying, she asked, "Why do you speak German among yourselves? Aren't you countrymen?"

"He's a Turk of necessity." Zelma meant me.

"No, by osmosis," I corrected her.

"I don't get it," the girl said.

"You know what osmosis is? It's the passage, voluntary or forced, of two liquids of different densities through a capillary wall. The Turks get called every name in the book, forcing them to pass through a wall of hatred. I am not Turkish, and ought therefore to pass through another capillary, but they put me in the same one."

"Good explanation, countryman. You ought to go into teaching," Zelma remarked.

"Too complicated for me. I still say you look like a Turk," the girl added, and left with her stuffed peppers.

The hot tea, sweet and fragrant, made me forget the cold. Two boys came in and ordered Thunder Kebab. Warming my hands on the glass of tea, I watched Zelma cut chunks of the golden roast lamb and stuff it into thin Turkish bread. She was as stout as a barrel, but she moved with the grace of a ballerina. I wondered if she ever did the belly dance, electrifying an audience of guys with mustaches. She had a white handkerchief over her black hair, and the childlike gleam in her eyes suggested that making a living was just a game to her. Generations of whores had eaten at Zelma's Imbiss. She gave them credit in lean times; some paid her in cash and some with insults, but Zelma never lost her good humor or the sparkle in her eyes.

"All right now, countryman. What are you going to have?"

"Something really good. It's my birthday."

"Ali," Zelma shouted, and from the back of the snack bar her husband, Ali, appeared, his eyes red from chopping onions.

Within minutes I was seated in front of a platter of fried eggplant, stuffed peppers, goat cheese, pepperoni, roast lamb, and delicate puff pastries with honey.

"I don't know how I'm going to eat all this," I said.

"With wine," Zelma said. "Ali, what are you waiting for?"

Ali uncorked a bottle of Portuguese wine and asked me how old I was. While stuffing myself, I told him.

"Forty-four," he started in, flicking his string of worry beads. "Forty-four. When I was your age I decided it was time to think of returning home. With our savings we could have opened a restaurant in Turkey, but Zelma, you know how she is, refused to leave the neighborhood. You ought to think about going home, kid. Time passes quickly, and you get left behind."

"Damn it, Ali, you want to throw me out of Germany too?"

Zelma's laughter filled the room. And when she stopped laughing, it was so the two of them together could serenade me with "Happy Birthday to You."

Out in the street it had begun to rain. The neon signs from the sex shops were reflected in the wet pavement. The pimps were making the rounds in their Mercedes sports cars, checking out the flesh exposed under umbrellas. I had just celebrated my birthday properly, or at least that's what the taste of the spices clinging to my palate told me. But Ali's words rang in my ears.

Go home, return. Return with wrinkles in your fore-head, and your hair gone gray at the temples. Return where? The only thing waiting for me in Chile was final proof that vengeance was impossible. No, that wasn't the only thing. There was someone, a person, a woman, who was waiting for me, maybe, or maybe she hadn't even no-ticed my absence because she herself was only absence and distance. How many times I had slapped myself, trying to force myself to face reality. Come on, I said to myself, here you are in Europe, in the West, in Germany, in Ham-burg, such and such latitude. But it was like slapping a defenseless reflection in a mirror, because my rebel neurons made it their business to remind me that I lived in that no man's land known, euphemistically, as exile.

You go into exile knowing only one side of the coin, and you hatch your same half-baked schemes outside the place where you conceived them. But once you've been through the tunnel and discovered that it's dark at both ends, you're caught, trapped like a fly on flypaper. There was no light at the end of the tunnel. It was just a feverish invention. And the place where you reside lets you see with surgical clarity that you are living in a region with no exit. And every passing year, instead of bringing you the seren-ity, wisdom, and cunning you need to try to escape, becomes one more link in the chain that binds you. And you can move, or think you do, you can advance in any direction, but the bigger your steps, the farther the border recedes, in geometric progression. No, Ali. I'll never get out of here, unless a miracle occurs, and we old guerrillas have neither the time nor the energy to latch on to new myths. It's hard enough tending the graves of our old ones. When all is said and done, Ali, what I'm afraid of is dying stark naked. For years I sought, like so many, the bullet with my name on it. It was the key to a dignified death, wearing the basic uniform of the true believer. But that's all finished. Belief faded away; our dogma was just an adolescent fantasy, and I was stripped bare of the one great expectation that set us apart, guys like me: dying for something called revolution. It was like the paradise reserved for Islamic holy warriors, but with salsa music.

The show had already started when I got to the Regina. On stage a girl was pretending to masturbate with a feather boa. I took my usual seat at the bar. Next to me Big Jim was stirring a concoction consisting of half a liter of milk, six eggs, a pinch of pepper, and a glass of rum. He drank it straight down and muttered Shit, the way he always did, and made a grimace to go with it. Before going on stage, he clapped me on the shoulder.

"Full house. I counted four johns total."

"A bad night, black man. Maybe things will pick up by the second show."

Big Jim was a bundle of muscles under a taut black patina. Wrapped in a cape of polyester leopard skin, he waited at one side of the stage for the emcee to introduce him.

"Respectable guests of the Regina, well, in a manner of speaking, no offense meant. Not quite respectable guests. Better, no? Straight from New Orleans, the American peep-show giant Big Jim Splash, the telepathic fucker!"

The four customers started hooting, as Jim came center stage, dragging a stool. He waited for the disc jockey to put on the first movement of *Also Sprach Zarathustra*. Then he took off his cape and stood there stark naked.

The four rubes were phonetically identifiable as Bavarians. For sure they didn't understand what was meant by a telepathic fucker. In guttural spasms they tried to explain that they had come to see bare-assed females, not males, much less black ones. But when Big Jim sat on the stool and began wriggling his hips so that all nine inches of his limp manhood swung from side to side, like a pendulum, there ensued the kind of respectful silence true artists appreciate.

"Rotten night. And I have to make the rent," said Tatiana the Pole.

"The cold keeps people away. Four johns," I answered.

"Five. There's a guy in a wheelchair in one of the reserved booths. I wanted to keep him company but he has a nasty dog that wouldn't let me."

I looked over at the reserved section and caught sight

of a man in a wheelchair. There was a champagne bucket on the table. The dog must have been underneath.

On stage, Jim, eyes shut, squeezed his hands and his buttocks. His cock had grown in size and was pointing its big dark head at the audience. Jim gritted his teeth and swung his hips in a series of undulating movements.

"Buy me a grappa? I'm flat broke," Tatiana complained.

"Just this one. You have to do your number. Look. The black is about to let the horses out of the barn."

"Damn him. I don't know how he does it. I took him to bed with me three times and it never worked. But did you see how he cheers up when there are women in the audience and they fight over who gets to fondle his prick?"

"You never asked me to sleep with you."

"Of course not. It must be because you're like a brother. And you don't screw your own brother. There's something monkish about you, did you know that? Don't get mad. Thanks for the grappa."

Big Jim's undulations had become a frenetic dance. Sweat was running down the telepathic fucker's face. All of a sudden he stood up, arms extended, clasped his hands behind his neck, and arched his back, to give his cock maximum extension. Then he let out a moan that came from the depths of his being, the slit in his glans dilated, and a geyser of semen erupted, hitting the empty tables in the front row.

The four customers did not applaud right away. One

of them boldly interrupted their Bavarian Catholic stupe-
faction to shout for an encore, but Big Jim was already
leaving the stage, dragging his synthetic leopard skin behind him. Now it was Tatiana the Pole's turn to perform.

"Straight from Warsaw, Tatiana the Polish jewel of
striptease. Persons with weak hearts should leave the room
before she removes her bra," the emcee was supposed to
say, but he didn't utter a word. He stood there, deathly
pale, and stared at the entrance. What I saw didn't exactly
delight me either.

Five monstrous babies. Shaved heads. T-shirts with the
slogan "I am proud to be German." Yankee bomber jack-
ets. Combat boots. They came in braying "Deutschland
über Alles" and belching a blue streak, their bellies and
their patriotism appropriately full of beer. When they finished braying the national anthem, one of them climbed
onto a table.

"Heil Hitler! From now on the laws of German mo-
rality will be obeyed in this stable. We hereby decree as
follows. Firstly: Decadent Filipinos, Poles, and blacks are
forbidden to display themselves in public, because they
offend German dignity. Secondly: It is forbidden for the
whores on duty to fuck foreign pigs. Thirdly: All members
of the artistic and service staff, including the women who
suck cock at the reserved tables, will pay fifty percent of
their income to the German People's Union, whose humble

representatives stand before you, to collect your donations. Heil Hitler!"

Having concluded their patriotic speech, they ordered a round of beers and warned us we'd better be nice to them, or they'd make a show of strength. And to make their meaning quite clear, they punched the barman in the face. So then it was my turn to open a dialogue with those babies. What the hell, that's what they paid me for.

I was on my way over to these Fourth Reich kids, with a conciliatory smile on my face, when, as luck would have it, I tripped over an invisible stair, fell forward, and banged my forehead against the jaw of the Nazi who had just been speechifying. Now it so happens I never studied pediatrics, but I knew that with babies you have to act fast, so while I consoled him for the teeth that got knocked out, by ramming him in the testicles with my knee a few times, I also led the chorus of Hamburg-by-night singers calling for the cops.

And they arrived. Preceded by screeching sirens, and with their innocent nine-millimeter Walthers drawn. The first thing they saw was the baby on the floor. The skinhead was slowly rediscovering the joy of breathing. With his body doubled up at right angles, he slapped at anyone who tried to move him.

"Who assaulted this man?" one of the cops asked.

"No one. They came in looking for a fight. Look what they did to my face," the barman said.

"That's a lie. We came in to have a beer and the Turk jumped us," one of the babies squealed.

"You, Turk. Show me your papers," ordered the cop in charge of this herd.

"Why?"

"Because I said so, damn it. Doesn't that sound like a good reason?"

You don't argue with the cops, especially when a whole team of them have their guns pointed at you. Slowly I put a hand into the inside pocket of my sports jacket and took out my passport, holding it with two fingers. The cop studied the blue cover of the passport. Maybe he didn't know his zoology and couldn't tell that the bird in the Chilean seal was a condor, not a hen; or that the little critter standing on its hind legs was a huemul, not a greyhound.

"Why do you have a Chilean passport?"

"Nobody gets to choose where they're born."

"I'm German and these pigs hit me. Or am I supposed to thank them for punching me?" the barman insisted.

"I'm a witness. They hit him with no warning," Tatiana corroborated.

"Name," said the cop.

"Tatiana Janowsky, Polish citizen."

"And you're not afraid of catching cold?" the cop asked, pointing to Tatiana's skimpy panties.

"I was going to do my gymnastics routine when this gang of pigs barged in," Tatiana insisted.

"She insulted us, you're witnesses. The minute we got into the place the wog jumped us," wailed another of the babies.

The cop who called the shots signaled for quiet and handed my passport to one of his underlings.

"See if this customer is clean, and call an ambulance for that one." He pointed to the baby who was whimpering on the ground.

"All right, let's have your version of what happened," he said to me.

"These guys came in, they insulted the house, they hit the barman, and I was about to ask them to leave when I tripped and banged into this gentleman. I'm terribly sorry. It was an accident."

"Of course. And his balls are up around his neck because he has hiccups. I'm afraid you'll have to come with us for routine questioning."

"Why? He was only trying to protect the reputation of the house," Big Jim said.

"Who's this creep?" the cop asked.

"Big Jim Splash. The telepathic fucker. American," the barman told him.

"Cover yourself up or I'll arrest you on a morals charge. And the Chilean comes with us to headquarters," the cop repeated.

This whole business was taking a nasty turn. German cops are terribly sensitive when you mess with their mental categories. Here was a clear-cut case of disorderly conduct, with a Turkish culprit served on a platter, but the Turk wasn't Turkish and he even had a German witness on his side. A bad business, the cop seemed to be thinking, and you didn't have to be a rocket scientist to guess what he had in mind. He wanted to lock me up in a cell for a few hours with the four babies, who were huddled together like comrades in misfortune.

"Hold out your hands," he ordered, showing me the handcuffs.

You have to know how to lose. I obeyed. Just at that moment, the man in the wheelchair spoke up. He spoke slowly, with a Swiss accent, from where he sat in the reserved section.

"Officer. Please come here for a moment. I think I can help you clear up this misunderstanding."

While the cop was talking with the cripple, the stretcher-bearers came in. They dodged the baby's slaps and kicks and examined him.

"Several teeth missing, possibly a broken nose. We'll get the rest from the X rays," one of them murmured, and they carried him out, still hunched up on the stretcher.

The cop in charge returned from the reserved section. I held out my hands but he ignored me.

"The passport," he said to the cop he had asked to check my record.

"He's clean," the other told him.

"OK. And you boys, go have fun somewhere else," he advised the babies.

"And what about me? My complaint? They hit me," the barman insisted once more.

"If you want to make a complaint, drop by headquarters. Good night."

Off they went. Just about then, the owner of the Regina ventured out of his office. The guy had monumental courage.

"You overdid it. A punch is a punch, but this time you went too far. Scandals like this drag down our reputation and scare away the clientele."

"Your help could not have come at a better time. Thanks."

"What was I supposed to do? I don't like to argue with the cops."

"Thanks all the same."

The barman patted his face with an ice cube. He scowled with contempt as the owner retreated to the safety of his office.

"Shall I pour you a drink?"

"A Jack Daniels with ice, but not that ice you're drooling on. Does it still hurt?"

"A little. You did a good job. That creep will be eating pabulum and farting out his neck, thanks to you. Too bad you didn't bust his balls. I didn't see any blood in his crotch."

"No one is perfect."

"The guy in the reserved section is signaling for you to come over."

I went over to his booth. The Bavarians had gone off, after the incident, which left him the only client. I figured he was about sixty; he had barely touched the champagne and he was smoking a fat cigar. When I got closer, the dog came out from under the table and bared his teeth at me.

"Down, Stinker. A glass of champagne?"

"I don't know what you told the cops, but I suppose I ought to thank you."

"Forget it. May I address you as a friend?"

"The customer is always right."

"You put on a pretty good show just now."

"Sometimes you're lucky. Sometimes not."

"Juan Belmonte. Did you know that's the name of a bullfighter?"

"I see you know my name."

"I know a lot about you. A whole lot."

"What's a disabled person like you doing in a joint like this?" The old man had that question coming. He was sitting in a wheelchair with an instrument panel full of control buttons, and he had on an elegant jacket. This old guy didn't buy his clothes on sale at C&A. His small hands were well manicured. At the opera you wouldn't have noticed him, but in a dive like the Regina he looked totally out of place. I could feel him sizing me up with his cynical smile the whole time. The dog was looking me over too.

"You called me. What do you want from me?"

"We need to have a long talk. In private, of course."

"There's a gay club ten yards down the block. Sorry, that's not my thing."

"Me a fag? Heavens no. Taking it up the ass in a wheelchair? I'd look like a steam shovel. And with a hard-on, I'd look like a tank. Heavens no."

He started laughing hard and then his deep smoker's cough took over. The dog was alarmed and began to growl menacingly.

"Down, Stinker. Nothing's the matter. We have to talk, Belmonte."

"That depends on the subject."

"About your past, for example. Don't disappoint me. I know you're Chilean and that Chileans are great conversationalists. I think it must come from the Indians. The Mapuches used to choose their chiefs in oratory contests."

"The Swiss are big talkers too. But I'm not interested in talking about my past or yours."

"Is my accent so strong? Oh well. Let's talk about work."

Work. It wasn't the first time someone had approached me with a proposition. A simple job, no complications, all you have to do is take some packages to Berlin, you understand? A white powder, a delicate detergent.

"I have a job and I like the work. Let's leave it at that. Good night."

"Wait, if you make one move, Stinker will tear your

balls off. You are going to work for me, Belmonte. I know everything there is to know about you. Everything. You don't believe me? I'll give you an example: two weeks ago you sent five hundred marks to Verónica."

His finger, his whole hand in the wound. I reached for him, intending to pick him up, wheelchair and all, but the dog got in the way. He was ready to lunge at my neck.

"Who the hell are you, rotten gimp?"

"You see how easy it is to talk. Down, Stinker. You are going to work for me and I assure you you will not regret it. Here's my card. We'll meet tomorrow at ten. Let's go, Stinker."

He shoved the table back and rolled his wheelchair to the exit. The dog arched his back, bared his teeth, and covered his master's retreat. I picked up the card. It showed a sailboat and three lines of text:

Oskar Kramer

Hanseatic Lloyd's

Overseas Investigations

"Belmonte," the cripple called to me from the door-way. "I almost forgot. Happy Birthday!"

The joint was empty. I returned to the bar. I could feel my back drenched with sweat. That cripple knew my most vulnerable point. I had to think, and fast. If anything had kept me going till now, it was knowing for certain that Veronica was out of danger, safe in her country of silence and oblivion. If the cripple knew about her, that

meant the machine that swallows men whole had not forgotten my name, my particulars, my moves, my habits.
Someone was reading the letters I received from Santiago,
learning about Veronica's condition, maybe discussing it
with colleagues in some secret room. That same someone
was reading my letters too, my words, the phrases of love
I sent month after month so they could be placed in her
lap, in hopes that suddenly one day she would ask for me
and my life would have meaning again. In that secret room,
the employees of the machine probably laughed at what
I'd written, and made obscene remarks while they drank
their beer and updated the file that kept track of every
move I made.

"The boss is calling you," the barman said.

He was sitting at his desk in a swivel chair, the wall
behind him full of photographs of cabaret performers. He
got right to the point.

"I don't like what you just did."

"You told me that before."

"I'm not talking about the skinheads. I'm talking about
the cripple. I saw the whole scene."

"It's a personal matter."

"I don't give a crap about your personal life. The cripple settled that mix-up with the cops. And you tried to
hit him. We won't be needing your services anymore. You
can't threaten or hit someone who's on good terms with
the cops."

"Am I fired?"

"Come around tomorrow and pick up what we owe you."

What a day. I'd been hit from all sides. When I got back to the bar, a dozen Japanese tourists were livening the place up. I checked the clock. It was almost midnight. Just as well my crummy birthday was winding down.

"Give me my last Jack Daniels," I told the barman.

"I heard everything. What a shit that guy is. If anything turns up, I'll let you know."

"Good luck, Turk," Big Jim murmured.

"Thanks, boys."

Outside it was raining hard. I turned up my coat collar and headed toward the docks. I had to act, get the advantage, anticipate events, but I didn't know how or where to begin. Suddenly, as I was walking along hugging the walls, I felt the weight of the coins in my pocket. Good thing I always carried a lot of spare change. Good thing I had this habit that kept the possibility of communication open at any time.

You dial two zeros and your wishes are lifted into outer space, where a satellite stores them, irrefutable evidence of the scientific future awaiting mankind. Two more digits transfer your anxieties from space to the southernmost shore of the Pacific; one more digit deposits them in the city of Santiago, and the final five digits carry them to the living room of a certain house.

"Hello, Señora Ana? Yes, it's me. I'm fine, fine. And

Verónica? The same. Yes. Still the same. Yes, please. See if she's awake."

Footsteps. In my memory, a door squeaked. The hinges need oiling, or tightening.

"She's awake? Please, hand her the phone. Verónica?"

I heard her regular breathing and said nothing. What could I say? It's me, love, Juan, and I'm talking to you although I know my voice doesn't reach you, no voice can reach you as long as you're lost in a labyrinth of horrors. Why don't you leave it, Verónica. Why don't you follow the stubborn example of your body, which emerged from the sea of disappearances after two years during which the machine tried to destroy it? Your naked body in a Santiago garbage dump, Verónica, my love.

"Juan. It's no good. She's not listening."

"All right, Señora Ana. I just wanted to know how she was."

"Same as always. She doesn't speak. She just goes on staring at something no one else can see. Juan . . . is something going on?"

"Why do you ask?"

"Because a couple of hours ago a friend of yours called asking how Verónica was doing. He said you'd be calling, and not to forget your appointment tomorrow. Was he a friend of yours, Juan?"

"Yes, a good friend, a great friend."

I had to act, take the offensive. What did that cripple

want? In desperation I started looking for his phone number in the directory. It wasn't listed. And just as I was about to dial information, a sudden cramp told me my intestines were shutting down.

I'm frightened. That's good. Fear impels you to think up a plan of action. You can still function, Juan Belmonte. There's nothing wrong with you, I told myself, walking the empty streets.

The lights were on in my apartment. I could see it from the street. There was no way the cripple could be waiting for me upstairs. The building had no elevator. I went up quietly and when I got to my door, I took off my belt. I opened the door, and holding the belt up with both hands, made my way to the living room. The little man in the ski cap was sprawled out, fast asleep.

"I hope you're comfortable," I greeted him.

Shorty woke with a start.

"Damn. I fell asleep. Sorry, boss."

"How long have you been here?"

"Since eight o clock. We couldn't repair the heating, so I brought you an electric heater. I sat down for a little while to wait for you, and I fell asleep. Forgive me."

He stood up, grabbed his toolbox, and headed reluctantly toward the door. He was short and tubby, and I've seen clams with longer necks.

"I'm sorry to bother you, but . . ."

"But you have to take the heater. Go ahead."

"No. I'm not going to leave you without heat. I missed the last subway train and I live way far out."

"All right. Stay here. I'll give you a blanket."

"Did you celebrate your birthday?"

"More or less."

Then Shorty opened his toolbox and took out a bottle of wine. He displayed it gleefully, like someone showing you a trophy he won.

"Let's polish it off," he suggested.

"There are glasses in the kitchen," I answered, remembering a proverb that says solitude is the worst place to look for advice.

CHAPTER FOUR

Berlin: Warrior's Wake-up Call

Frank Galinsky opened the door of the apartment and came face-to-face with solitude. He turned on the living-room light. The bare walls, with their empty rectangles where paintings once hung, struck him as unfair, outrageous. Without furniture, the room looked enormous. He went through the apartment, turning on all the lights. In Jan's room only a few rock posters were left to show that till just a few days ago his son had lived here. Shutting the door, he discovered a rubber bone. How would Blitz, the German shepherd, manage without his toy? Helga had taken everything, the furniture, Jan, even the dog. He gave the bone a kick and went to the kitchen, where he had arranged the meager furnishings Helga left him. His worldly possessions consisted of a folding cot, a table, and a chair. They looked even sadder all crammed into the kitchen, where he slept now, to save on the heating.

He set the chair by the kitchen window, took a can of beer from a plastic bag, and with his feet propped on the radiator, sat staring into the street. Soon the day's first tram would pull up at the empty stop. Soon morning would come. Soon winter would be over. Soon the incomparable Berlin spring would arrive. Soon . . .

To tell the truth, everything was happening too fast in Frank Galinsky's life. Suddenly, he had become a citizen of the Federal Republic of Germany, without having to defect to the enemy camp, because just as suddenly the German Democratic Republic had disappeared. It had vanished, evaporated, deflated, without struggle or glory, its demise totally devoid of the exaggerated, megalomaniac theatrics that marked its existence as a nation. For East Germans, the joy of stuffing themselves with bananas was suddenly passé, and they were learning how to keep up with the happy life they'd been hearing, intuiting, smelling for four decades on the other side of that damned wall. Now was the time to request, to demand, to possess everything. The longing to satisfy repressed curiosity governed even their taste buds. Plain vanilla or chocolate ice cream was no longer enough for them. No, now they demanded exotic flavors: pineapple, mango, papaya, passion fruit. His own son had startled him by asking if there was such a thing as avocado ice cream. Yes indeed. Everything had changed suddenly, and would go on changing.

Frank Galinsky lit a cigarette of Virginia tobacco, the kind you could buy anywhere now. American cigarettes.

Not that crap he had smoked for four decades, nothing but dry straw. How lucky that the Major was looking for him, because when such rapid changes are occurring, it's good to align yourself with those who decide what direction those changes will take.

When the wall fell, chapter one in the silent extinction of the proletarian state, Galinsky felt a disturbing symptom he soon recognized as fear, a different fear from the sensation he had known on "international missions" to Angola, Cuba, Mozambique, or Nicaragua. As an officer in the German People's Army, and what's more an intelligence officer, he had belonged to the elite who enjoyed the favors of the state, and there is no fear more terrible than not knowing when or how or by whom the bill for favors received is likely to be presented.

The old institutions crumbled overnight. The army of the GDR was disbanded, its uniforms and medals bartered at flea markets for solid German marks. Its soldiers remained "on call" while their conduct in the service of the defunct communist regime was under investigation.

To be "on call" meant you were under suspicion. It was the equivalent of suffering from a contagious disease, under strict quarantine. The first symptom was that old friends refused to greet you, former comrades, the same bastards who used to line up with their shopping lists every time you were due to travel abroad.

Helga too was infected by the disease. She lost her job

as an art teacher, because "As you know, Mrs. Galinsky, your husband is under investigation. Of course if you decide to cooperate with the occupation, sorry, the reunification authorities, and alert them to certain facts your husband may have forgotten . . ."

The disease soon spread to their apartment. A man showed up, just dropped by, unannounced, surrounded by police and shyster lawyers.

"What do you mean, you own it? This is my apartment. I have the papers to prove it. It was sold to me by the state."

"A bunch of garbage, Herr Galinsky. This apartment house was built illegally, on a lot that belongs to our client. We can show you copies of the deeds to prove it. They date from the Weimar Republic. Time is money, Herr Galinsky. Sign this rental contract, or we'll have to start eviction proceedings."

His unemployment check was barely enough to make ends meet. Helga had to take a job as a salesgirl in a dress shop, while Galinsky clenched his fists every time he passed the Labor Exchange.

"Name: Frank Galinsky Age: forty-four. Profession: soldier. List your specialties: Scuba diving instructor, martial arts teacher. Languages: Spanish, Portuguese, Russian, and English. Interesting. Ah, but you're currently "on call." We'll be in touch with you. When your case is cleared up."

You're forty-four years old and a former intelligence officer in the army of the GDR. What the hell do you do next? Galinsky spent six months belaboring the question, standing by that same kitchen window, drinking the same brand of beer, and staring vacantly at the same trolley-car stop he had his eye on now.

Looking out that same window one evening he saw a BMW park outside his door. An elegant guy with artfully tousled gray hair got out and slipped gracefully around to the other side of the car, to open the passenger door. The passenger was Helga. Smiling, she exchanged a few words with the driver. Galinsky couldn't hear what was being said. The man kept stroking her arm the whole time, and when he said good-bye, he kissed her hand.

"Who's your chauffeur? I didn't know the shop had its own limousine service," Galinsky greeted Helga as she was hanging up her overcoat.

"He's the owner of the shop. A very attentive gentleman."

"I'll say. He had his paws all over you."

"Don't be vulgar."

"Don't be a whore. The droit du seigneur went out with feudalism. Or have you forgotten history, too?"

Helga stared at him coldly. Her blue eyes laughed. She let out the words slowly, as if she'd been rehearsing them through long sleepless nights.

"No. I haven't forgotten history. On the contrary. I'm

just beginning to understand it. In case you haven't noticed yet, I've been working all day, earning money, so that among other things we can pay the rent on this crummy apartment, while all you do is drink beer and complain all day long. That man who just dropped me off is my boss and he has fantastic plans for my future. He's opening a new store and he wants me to manage it. Do you understand? It's my future, and Jan's, and maybe even yours."

Galinsky's open hand slammed into his wife's face. She tottered, grabbed the back of a chair, and fell over with it. His first impulse was to help her up, but Helga waved him away.

She stood up, straightened her dress, and shut herself in the bedroom.

Galinsky tried to get in, but the door was locked.

"Helga, I'm sorry. I didn't mean to hurt you. Helga."

After a few minutes, she opened the door. She was carrying a small overnight bag.

"What does this mean? Where are you going?"

"None of your business. Let me by."

"Helga. I said I was sorry. Don't be vindictive."

"I'm not, Frank. I'm actually grateful to you. You gave me the impetus I needed. I'm leaving you and I'm taking our son with me. I've given it a lot of thought, and if I didn't leave sooner, maybe it's because I still have some leftover notion of loyalty, solidarity, all that crap they brainwashed us with. But I also know you have to be a winner, no matter what. There's no place for failures in the new Germany. That's the truth, pure and simple."

"You take one step, one little step, and I'll break every bone in your body."

"You touch a hair on my head and I'll reveal your terrorist connections. You think I'm stupid? You think I don't know what they're investigating in your past? Have you forgotten those trips to Africa and Central America? Let me by, Frank. It's best this way for both of us."

"Get out before I kill you."

Helga got out. A week later she came back with a lawyer to retrieve her possessions and their son's. She took the dog too. The next time he saw her was five months later, when they were summoned to court to sign divorce papers.

What damn good is a former intelligence officer of an army that was defeated without ever going into battle? Galinsky couldn't find an answer to his question. He had been gnawing at it for two hours, sitting on a bench near the exit of Jan's school, when a man sat down beside him.

"Why the long face, Galinsky? No one has any reason to be sad in unified Germany," the Major greeted him.

Galinsky had never been close to the Major, but he had known him since the late seventies, when the Major headed a clandestine military school that gave courses in sabotage, intelligence, and logistics to several dozen African and Latin American revolutionaries, men chosen to form the officer corps in the future armed forces of their respective countries. The Major himself taught the Latin Americans.

"What a surprise. How are you, Major?"

"Fine, thanks. Can you say the same?"

Galinsky took a good look at him. He had to be nearly sixty, but he looked younger without that cloddish, rat gray uniform. He had on a well-cut dark suit and kidskin gloves. He gave off that subtle aura of expensive aftershave and well-being you find in men of the ruling class.

"I'm in a bad way, Major. Real bad."

"I've heard something. But I want to know your version."

Old fox, Galinsky thought. This chance meeting is nothing of the sort. He's up to the same old tricks. In this corner, we have the legion of brave warriors, the tried and true, capable of carrying out any mission at the front. But for the really difficult operations, slipping a man past the enemy lines, heroes aren't worth a cup of warm spit. For that, you appeal to some poor slob who doesn't stand out in the first ranks, the kind who wounds a dead horse with his sword so he can show he's drawn blood when the battle's over. Tell me your troubles, says the officer. Let's put rank aside and talk man to man. And the guy lets loose, reveals his weaknesses. The officer pretends to sympathize, meanwhile keeping careful count. The poor guy is taking an intelligence test, without knowing it. And finally, after his every sign of good sense has been turned into a sin, he's generously offered a chance to make amends, to rehabilitate himself through penitence. All he has to do is make a little pilgrimage behind enemy lines. It's wise to select your volunteers from among those least suited for heroic action, or those most affected by wartime disruptions of civilian life. You were one clever bastard, von Clausewitz.

"I'm finished. On call. Out of work. Divorced. And in two weeks I have to give up my apartment. *Kaputt*, Major, *kaputt*."

"I know. But life could improve, Frank Galinsky, my old comrade in the Latin American section. Are you ready to accept an assignment?"

"I'd do anything to get out of this mess."

"No questions asked?"

"All a soldier needs to know are his destination and his objective."

"Things are looking up for you already, Galinsky. Tomorrow you have a business dinner with me. I'll pick you up at eight on our dear Alexanderplatz, by the clock that shows the time all over the world."

Frank Galinsky greeted his son, ruffling the boy's hair. He took his schoolbag and slung it over his shoulder. And so they covered the five blocks between school and Helga's apartment. He kissed his son good-bye at the door of the apartment.

"Jan? Remember I promised you one day we'd go for a vacation in Spain? Well, we're going to be going, and soon."

"Really? Do they have pioneer camps in Spain? What about Blitz? Can we take him?"

"Of course. Of course the dog will go with us."

After he left Jan, he took a long walk through the city. He was elated, he felt his life was beginning again. Suddenly he caught his reflection in a shop window.

"You look awful, comrade, really awful. If you want to go back to being what you once were, you'd better start now," he muttered, and began jogging toward the shore of the Wannsee.

He went on jogging round and round the lake, until night fell, until the last house along the shore turned out its lights, until his muscles rebelled, until he was sure that he could still dominate them, conquer his body, until he looked at his watch and saw that it was four in the morning.

When he stopped running, his body was bathed in sweat. He had expelled the shame of defeat, through every pore.

CHAPTER FIVE

Hamburg: A Stroll by the Elbe

I was awakened by a cramp in my right leg. Grabbing for it, I opened my eyes and saw I was lying on the sofa. Close by, on the coffee table, were a thermos, fresh rolls, and a jar of marmalade.

"Good morning, boss," Shorty greeted me. Without his ski mask, and with his wet hair slicked back, he looked more like a runt than ever. He had just taken a shower.

"What time is it?"

"Seven-thirty, boss. Looks like the wine got to you last night. You passed out on the floor and I didn't want to disturb you. Shall I pour your coffee? There are fresh rolls."

"Where did you sleep?"

"In your bed, boss, but on top of the covers. Don't worry, I didn't get the sheets dirty. I just didn't want to bother you. And now I'm leaving because the contractor must be on his way. Today for sure we'll get the heat back on. See you later."

He put on his blue ski cap, grabbed his toolbox, and headed for the door.

"Wait. You must have a name, no?"

"Pedro de Valdivia. Well, actually my name is Pedro Valdivia, and I added the 'de' myself. It sounds classier, don't you think?"

"Great. Listen, Pedro de Valdivia. I want to ask you a favor."

"Just say the word."

"There's a possibility someone will phone while you're in the apartment. If they ask for me, tell them I left on a trip and you don't know when I'll be back. Same thing if they come snooping around. Got it?"

"Woman trouble, boss?"

"Worse. Can you do me that favor?"

"He left yesterday and I have no idea when he'll be back."

"That's it. Thanks, big guy."

In the shower I began to analyze the situation mechanically: (a) The cripple was not with the cops; cops in wheelchairs only happen in the movies. (b) He was on good terms with the cops or, rather, with someone upstairs, at whatever level. (c) In addition to his relations with the cops, he also had contacts in the Constitutional Defense

Service, the political police of the German federation. They were the only ones who could have given him information about me. His knowing about Verónica proved it. I had always assumed that as an exile, I was in Big Brother's memory bank, but I never thought they considered me important enough to mess with my letters and money orders. I was what they called a transparent man. (d) The cripple was not a member of the political police, since he had told me to meet him at an insurance company office. Even if the office was a front, why blow his cover letting someone like me know about it? Besides, if the political police wanted something from me, to use me as an informer, for example, they wouldn't have come looking for me in a public place. Conclusion: none. What the hell did the cripple want with me?

Out in the street I realized how long it had been since I'd seen morning light. It was just short of nine A.M. I took out the card the cripple gave me and saw that no address was given. I didn't like that. The old guy had thrown out the only bait I was likely to swallow: Verónica. But then he gave me an appointment at an unspecified address. What was his game? I looked up the address of Hanseatic Lloyd's in the phone book. It wasn't far, near the docks. I decided to walk there.

Walking at that hour, I saw the city in a whole new way. It was cold. The trees were bare; their trunks were covered with green moss, rather shiny, intensely green. The copper roofs of Hamburg's typical buildings were green too. I liked this city, the way we like meeting up again with someone who has protected us, sheltered us, and encouraged us from time to time. The prospect of having to shove off again was painful.

It was a familiar pain. I remembered what a nice life I had in Cartagena de las Indias, after my last political failure. I worked as a proofreader for a magazine, which left me free to enjoy the superb Caribbean sunsets, until one evening, when I was held up, very persuasively, by a couple of guys with their guns pointed at my gut.

This is the end of the road for me, I thought, taking them for members of some death squad that had been given my name, for whatever reason.

"Easy, big guy. You have nothing to worry about," one of them said.

"Someone wants to have a drink with you. And since it's news to you, we're going to take you there. Don't try to act tough, big boy," the other one said.

My escorts took me to a restaurant in downtown Cartagena. There I was greeted by a man they called the Attorney. He offered me a whisky, Chivas. I turned him down.

"You don't like whisky?" the Attorney asked.

"Yes, but I only drink Jack Daniels, with ice."

The Attorney shook his head and spoke to his bodyguards.

"A Sandinista comandante who drinks gringo whisky. What do you make of that?"

"Chivas is a real man's drink," one of them pointed out.

"In Colombia we're all real men, Chilean. What about in your crummy country?"

"Half of us are real men and the other half are real women. It works out pretty well that way, half and half."

I had scored one against the two escorts. They muttered, "Don't overdo it," but the Attorney told them to keep quiet.

"I like a man with guts, but let's cut the crap. Listen, Belmonte, Juan Belmonte—how do you like that, he has the same name as Hemingway's bullfighter. Listen. Someone upstairs wants you to work for him. Do you know Medellín? It's a pretty town and the streets are paved with dollars, but it could use a little law and order. Someone upstairs thinks a man of your experience would be perfect for the job. You follow me?"

"Can I think it over?"

"Upstairs says you already thought it over."

"Of course. I forgot. When do I leave for upstairs?"

"Tomorrow. The boys will keep you company till then. Upstairs doesn't want you getting lost."

Blessed be the five commandments of clandestinity, which make it easier for her beloved sons to move around: (1) Know which bars have windows in the john; (2) rent a P.O. box, and keep your papers and your few valuables there; (3) always have an airline ticket ready, on the domestic airline, to the largest city in the region; (4) be sure to spell out your name loud and clear, so it will show up on the passenger list; (5) be generous to the little whore you've chosen for a mistress, and never ask anything shameful of her in return.

Noble whore. She helped me to leave Cartagena on a tramp steamer crossing the Caribbean. Leaving the Gulf of Darien behind, while the Attorney's men waited for me at the Bogotá airport, I said farewell to Cartagena and the dream of a quiet, forgotten life by the sea, as in the poem of Gil de Biedma, "like a ruined nobleman living among the ruins of my mind."

Sure it hurt to leave the Caribbean, but between becoming a hired killer for a drug dealer or a trophy for Colombian soldiers eager to pose with the corpse of a foreign extremist, life always offers a third alternative: you can simply vanish.

What the hell. Maybe it was time for me to leave Hamburg. I had an open ticket to Costa Rica and in my P.O. box I had two thousand dollars in cash. I could take off in any direction, but the problem was Verónica, alone, incapable of looking after herself, back in Santiago.

Here I come, Oskar Kramer. You've got me on a tight leash. You may know my life by heart, but there's one thing you don't know. I know how to lose. That's a great advantage in these times, I said to myself as I headed toward the offices of Hanseatic Lloyd's.

"The basic rule of conduct before combat: The guerrilla knows that he is facing an enemy who is better equipped militarily. He must strike once, forcefully, definitvely, and then fall back. He should be calm and relaxed when he goes into combat, certain that he has made the correct analysis of the forces involved. He should know that nature will help him achieve the serenity indispensable to the guerrilla." Commander Giap.

Old Vietcong SOB, old humbug. But I followed his advice. A few minutes later it began raining hard. I decided I would try to relax by stepping up the pace while thinking about an umbrella. I would buy a Japanese umbrella, the latest model, with a sensor that could detect when its owner moved more than a yard out of range. At that point a robot voice would shout, "Don't forget me." Did such a marvel exist? The Japanese were idiots if they hadn't already invented such a useful object. The unlosable umbrella. The umbrella with a built-in alarm. The umbrella that refused to open for anyone but its owner.

Well then, I had managed to think about something else, but the Hamburg air still emitted a familiar stench: the awful smell of cut and run.

The receptionist at Lloyd's, the world's largest maritime insurance company, according to the bronze plaque on the door, looked at me with the same interest he would have shown a turd on the sidewalk.

"Good morning. I have an appointment with Oskar Kramer," I said.

"Do you speak German?"

"I have an appointment with Mr. Kramer. At ten."

"I asked you if you speak German."

"I don't think we're speaking Afrikaans."

"Your ID."

"Kramer is expecting me at ten."

"Identification."

I handed him my Chilean passport. He regarded it with disgust. Now that he knew my name, he checked his list.

"You have an appointment with Mr. Kramer at ten."

"You don't say. What a pleasant surprise."

"You think you're funny?" He nailed me with a stare.

I accepted his challenge and began to study the glint of light from the street reflected in his eyes. So Kramer had an office in this building. He left me his card, minus an address, sure I would look for it. The guy lowered his gaze and pretended to look for something on his desk. I felt sorry for him. A frustrated puppet, miserable in his humble blue subaltern's uniform. What he would have liked was a uniform dripping decorations, visible proof of his power to decide who got into the Lloyd's building and who didn't. He started jotting down some of the basics, flipping through the pages of my passport with an expression on his face that went from disgust to astonishment.

I was messing with his mental categories. Call that a passport, this little booklet with its incomprehensible seal, adorned with two critters that might well have been a chicken and a rat on its hind legs, instead of the powerful German eagle, with wings outstretched. Yes indeed, I was messing with his mind. He was probably wondering how a guy who looked like a foreigner could travel the world without a Turkish passport.

"Wait here. I'll call you at five to ten and give you a visitor's pass," he barked, pointing to a corner of the lobby.

I stuffed myself into a leather chair and lit a cigarette. I glanced at the table and the inevitable potted rubber plant, and then went back to the receptionist.

"I ordered you to wait there."

"Take it easy, Fritz. Do you have an ashtray?"

"Smoking is not permitted, and my name is not Fritz."

"Then we have three problems. One, your name isn't Fritz, although that's a perfectly nice name. Two, I'll have to smoke outside; and three, you'll have to come out to get me when it's five to ten."

Smoking in the doorway, I felt surprisingly calm. Kramer, whoever he was and whatever he did, was doubtless one powerful guy and yet I was not afraid of him. Sometimes you just have to confront these dead-end situations. Kramer knew about Verónica. Knowledge is power, according to McLuhan. And that combination, joined to a desire to do harm, can be terrifying. I was afraid for her, yet I was as calm as a statue. Suddenly I felt like the character in Ring Lardner's "Champion," a boxer who has to win a match not for himself, but for the army of defenseless souls who depend on his fists.

I ground out the cigarette butt as the receptionist knocked on the glass door.

"Mr. Kramer is waiting for you. Room 505. Keep your pass visible at all times," he said, handing me a rectangle of plastic. I put it in my pocket.

While waiting for the elevator, I took out a cigarette.

"I told you, smoking is not allowed," the receptionist squealed from his corner.

"I'm not smoking."

"And wear your pass where it can be seen."

"This is an English flannel jacket. It doesn't take any decorations. What would the Queen say?"

"The rules must be obeyed."

"On that we can agree, Fritz," I said, and got into the elevator.

Kramer's office was large and cold. On one wall was a bulletin board with some papers tacked to it. There was nothing to be seen on his desk but a black telephone, a rotary model. The fluorescent lighting added to the chilly atmosphere. He pointed to the only available chair.

"Belmonte, Juan Belmonte. Why did they give you that name? Last I heard, Chileans were not great bullfight fans."

"Nor am I. Is that what you want to discuss with me?"

"No. To set your mind at ease, let me start by saying I'm going to play clean with you, as clean as my own interests permit. As you already know, my name is Oskar Kramer and I'm Swiss. My official title is Department Head, Overseas Investigations for Hanseatic Lloyd's. Before that I was with the police, in Zurich, until an arms dealer gave orders to have a slug of lead inserted in my spine."

"A sad story. What does it have to do with me?"

"You'll find out. All in due time. I'll try not to act like a typical Swiss. We are famous for our slowness, you know. Juan Belmonte. Like the great bullfighter. My contacts with the German authorities are generally quite useful. Did you know you're listed with the PDPs, potentially dangerous persons? They gave me a copy of your resume. Interesting, Belmonte. Very interesting. Guerrilla in Bolivia at the time of the National Liberation Army offensive in Teoponte. Urban guerrilla in Chile. Took part in several bank robberies, or as they say in militant circles, 'expropriations.' Participated in several terrorist attacks in the first years of the resistance against the Pinochet regime. Another interesting detail. Military service in a Chilean commando unit. Two stays in Cuba, tourist in Angola and Mozambique, guerrilla in Nicaragua, Simón Bolívar International Brigade. Then Sandinista comandante. This is much too interesting a career for a brothel goon, and one named after a bullfighter, to boot."

"Come on, Big Brother. Tell me what you know about Verónica."

"Very little. Mentioning her was a trick, a dirty trick, I grant you. I suppose I ought to apologize."

"You said you'd play clean. Out with it, what do you know about Verónica?"

"As you wish. Her resume is brief. Until 1973, active in the Socialist Youth organization. Arrested in October 1977 by agents of the National Security Directorate in Santiago. Listed as missing in January '78, but in July 1979 a couple of tramps find her in a garbage dump on the south side of the city. A medical exam by the Human Rights Commission reveals that she has been tortured extensively. From the day she was found she's been mentally incompetent. Another medical report mentions a form of schizophrenia better known as autism. Then we have her current address, phone number, and, finally, mention of the fact that she's your only contact in Chile. There are photocopies of every letter you sent her. That's all."

"Those bastards who collect my letters, are they plain old cops, or something classier?"

"I play clean with them too, so I can't tell you, but . . ."

"Go ahead. You still haven't told me what you want from me."

"But I can destroy both your file and hers, and I assure you there are no copies."

"You're bluffing. You know they can't touch Verónica. Chile is no longer a dictatorship, and even if it were, they have nothing on her."

"Not on her, directly, but what would happen if I had you expelled from Germany? She's dependent on you. On the money you send her. I had you followed, Belmonte. You live very frugally. You even roll your own cigarettes. And I'm told Verónica has no one, except that aunt who looks after her. I believe her name is Ana. Your loyalty to a woman you haven't seen since 1973 is admirable, unless you continued to meet after you went underground in Chile. Admirable."

"I'm getting tired of this, Kramer. Just tell me what the hell you want from me."

"All in due time. Let's go for a walk. You'll push the wheelchair, incidentally, I'll economize on batteries, and meanwhile I'll dangle my hook with a nice juicy bait. In the end, you'll bite."

We left the building. The receptionist was all smiles when he saw me with Kramer and that repulsive dog jumping for joy at the prospect of a walk. We set out along the bank of the Elbe, and I thought, One little shove would be enough to make him disappear in its filthy waters.

We walked all the way to the Blankenesse gardens. Kramer watched the ships entering and leaving the harbor and spoke of fortunes, great works of art, collections of priceless objects lost before, during, and after the Second

World War. I listened, struggling against the temptation to heave him into the river. The dog seemed to have telepathic powers, because he kept on looking at me and baring his teeth.

"And the big losers in all these stories of missing treasure were not the owners, but the insurance companies, Belmonte. No sooner was the last shot in the Second World War fired than the Cold War began, in 1945, although historians insist it all started when they built the Berlin Wall. The year 1945, when the map of Europe was split between Red and White, fell like a guillotine for the insurance companies, cutting the series of clues that, tied together, would have shown the way to many of the missing treasures. But the insurers all knew that sooner or later the links of the chain would join up again, that logical continuity would be restored, leading to closure, the inevitable completion of the circle."

"What the hell kind of Chinese is that? I can't understand a word you're saying."

"All right. To make a long story short: For more than forty years, on both sides of the wall, fragments of stories were preserved. Everyone was sure that on the other side, people who knew something would wait patiently for the propitious moment to put all the bits and pieces together. That moment came with the collapse of the socialist world. Now the circles began to close, but with such dizzying speed that they threatened to form spirals."

"You're getting on my nerves, Kramer. You said you'd

play clean, and instead you keep entangling me in these parables that make no sense to me. What's it to me if your fucking circles close or stay open? And tell your damn dog to stop rubbing against my legs. Don't you ever give him a bath?"

"Stinker's personal hygiene is his own business. Wheel me over to that café. I haven't had breakfast yet."

The Elbe Lookout café was empty at that hour. We took a table by the window. Outside, a steady stream of ships passed by. On many of them you could see the crew on deck, busy with their outward-bound chores. I envied them. Soon they would reach Cuxhaven and the freedom of the open sea. Kramer ordered coffee and scrambled eggs. The dog got a great big sausage.

"Eat up, Belmonte. Meanwhile I'll tell you a story, to help you understand why I need you. Listen. When it was only a matter of time till the Berlin Wall collapsed, the East Germans were all out celebrating in advance. They paraded around shouting 'We are one people,' they cleared their palates for the taste of Coca-Cola, all except one little old man. Let's call him Otto. All over South America they tell Don Otto jokes, right? Now then, our Don Otto, former member of Hitler's SS and subsequently hero of labor in the German Democratic Republic, skipped the celebrations and planted himself like a fence post, just across from the legendary Checkpoint Charlie. And there he waited day and night. Rigid as a sentry in the old days.

He got cramps, he had to pee, but he held out, waiting for the historic moment when the People's Police began selling their uniforms and their medals to the reporters. The German Democratic Republic was dead. And then, as Berliners from both sides of the city rushed to embrace one another and tear down the wall with their bare hands, our Don Otto ran to the first phone booth he could find in the West, dialed Information, asked for the number of Hanseatic Lloyd's in Hamburg, rang them up, and asked to speak with the top boss. I imagine Don Otto must have felt somewhat frustrated when he was told to call back the next day, but a man who has waited more than forty years to play his hand can't waste time. Don Otto insisted. He said, 'Find the top boss at home, or wherever he is, and just tell him Kunsthalle, Bremen, 1945. He'll understand. I'll call back in an hour.'

"Magic words, Belmonte. The President of Lloyd's showed up at the office in his pajamas at eleven that night. Less than two hours later, Don Otto was settling his ass into a limousine that whisked him from Berlin to Hamburg. At six A.M. he was received with honors by the president of the company and a pack of historians and art experts. Several employees of Lloyd's got no sleep that night. Now here's the point, Belmonte. Don Otto drank a cup of coffee and said, 'You are looking for the missing collection from the Bremen Kunsthalle. I know where it is. Let's talk about the reward.' In case you hadn't heard, this magnificent collection of paintings is valued at sixty million dollars.

" 'Our research suggests that it may be in Moscow,' said a historian. Don Otto didn't bat an eyelash.

" 'Could be. But only part of it,' he said, and then he told his story. He'd had a hand in the disappearance of the paintings. Once the question of the reward was settled, he grew more talkative. A large part of the collection was now in Asunción, Paraguay, in safekeeping with a former SS comrade-in-arms whose identity and address would be worth gold in Israel. To make his point more forcefully, Don Otto showed them some photographs which, although of very poor quality, had the experts trembling with emotion.

"Don Otto began to see a rosy future for himself. Accompanied by Lloyd's executives and art experts, he flew across the Atlantic. During the crossing he must have thought about what he would do with the reward, about the value of patience as a virtue, but on landing in Asunción his dreams degenerated into hellish nightmares. The Paraguayan papers just then were full of the story of the tragic death of a distinguished member of the German colony in Asunción. Apparently, he was the victim of an accident in his bathtub. A hair dryer, left running, fell into the bathwater and shocked him into the next world. An accident, you follow me?"

"I saw something like that in a James Bond movie. With a fan. What happened to the paintings?"

"No one knows where they are now. They may turn up. Most likely they'll wind up in the air-conditioned cellars of some Arabian collector."

"Let's have the punch line to your Don Otto joke."

"I don't think he found it very funny. We paid for his return trip and handed him over to the police. After all, in 1945 he was accomplice to a theft that was harmful to our interests at Lloyd's. You understand the moral of the story?"

"The best laid plans of mice and men . . . They got to Paraguay too late. But I still don't understand why you're telling me all this and what you want from me."

"I need your experience and your resourcefulness, for an investigation. So we don't get to Paraguay, or wherever, too late."

"You're crazy. What do I know about investigations? I should think a company like Lloyd's works with the best detectives. And tell your damn dog to leave my trousers alone."

"I think he likes you. You think correctly. We have the best detectives, investigators, but they never leave the lab or the library. They do their research with computers. Actually, it's not that difficult to locate a work of art or a precious object. It just takes patience. The real difficulties come later, with the give and take, the bribes, with rules dictated by the law of supply and demand. That's what determines whether an object will change hands. That's how it is in normal times, but as you know, Belmonte, times are changing rapidly. The rules of the game have changed too. Now we have to conduct our investigations with very few leads, we have to do our tracking, locate what we're looking for, and act fast. Don't make that face, I'm getting to the point. This is what you need to know. You have no idea, no one has any idea, how much loot we've recovered from South America. For forty-something years we negotiated with the Third Reich boys rescued through the Odessa connection. It was slow, painful work, strictly for bureaucrats, but we could do it because we had lots of time. But now the inhabitants of the socialist world are no longer locked up. The borders have opened and there's nothing to stop those who have secret information from going after what they think belongs to them. And as most of them have gotten older, they either sell their secrets to the highest bidder or rush into the field. They want their cut now."

"I still don't see where the hell I fit into the picture."

"Think of a character like Mengele. Banned and hunted by half the world, and yet he managed to live happily and legally between Brazil and Paraguay. The Jews were never able to prove to a Brazilian or Paraguayan court that that harmless-looking old guy who'd been photographed thousands of times was the Angel of Death himself. So they tried to lay hands on him by other means, as they did with Eichmann in Buenos Aires, but it didn't work. They sent several commandos to kidnap or eliminate

Mengele, but they all failed, and do you know why? Because they didn't know how to function outside the law in South America. You do, Belmonte. You've mastered the art of clandestinity. A former guerrilla from the southern tier is not the romantic failure portrayed in the Social Democratic press. The triumph of capitalism has made guerrilla know-how a precise and much needed science, for the time being. Now then, what do I want from you? Your experience."

The cripple had finished talking. He stared at me with a smug expression. How could I have been afraid of such an idiot? Talk about a stuffed shirt. If Kramer, with his absurd notions about guerrillas, was respected by the political police, no wonder they had never caught up with the fugitives from the Baader-Meinhof gang.

"Experience. You don't know what you're talking about. You don't understand a damn thing. I don't deny I was mixed up in a couple of adventures, but they were failures, Kramer. Failures. Go take a look in Paris, or Berlin, and you'll find hundreds of retired guerrillas."

"Of course. But a man who fired a few shots in the jungle is not the same as one who's been all over the map. Did you know the German antiterrorist police study the Somoza assassination? They consider it a real gem. Five men manage to slip into the most heavily guarded country in South America, Paraguay, where one in four inhabitants is a police informer. They smuggle arms into the country, even a couple of rocket launchers. They catch up with Somoza and terminate him. And they weren't from Nicaragua, Belmonte. They were from the southern cone. Guys like you. I've been looking for an ex-Tupamaro for a long time, an ex–People's Revolutionary Army soldier, someone like you, who knows languages, sabotage techniques, the underground, invisibility; someone who's been all over the world and has left a network of contacts behind in every country."

"You're crazy, Kramer. What you're saying is a romantic fantasy. The man you need is called Iván Ilich Ramírez. I'll make you a gift of his name."

"The legendary Carlos. Don't think I didn't consider him. Too bad he's an old man. When they threw him out of Lebanon he moved to Syria with his harem of German girls. The ladies of the Red Army Faction like to screw. They wore him to shreds. He's useless. Let's finish up. You are going to work for me. Not for Lloyd's. For me."

"No. Neither for Lloyd's nor for you. Anything else?"

"Yes, there's something else. You ought to know that the police received an anonymous tip that led them to a consignment of cocaine. While you were waiting in our lobby at Lloyd's, they were searching your place. A nasty business, Belmonte, because your accomplice, a guy named Valdivia, resisted the break-in. A bad business. Two thousand dollars in your post office box? It's been confiscated. That's standard in cases like this. Don't get nervous. Stinker likes people to be relaxed."

"You bastard, you thought of everything."

"Of course. We Swiss don't like to leave loose ends. It's a national deformation. And now let's get out of here. We'll head back slowly. The police need time to recognize their error."

"What do I have to do?"

"Travel. To Chile. You're going home, Belmonte. And don't think about deserting. You know very well that extradition between your country and Germany functions beautifully."

"You win, for now. But you'll pay me for this, Kramer. I don't know how, but I'm going to mess you up."

"Have you seen *Casablanca*? At the end of the movie the French policeman tells Rick, 'I think this may be the beginning of a beautiful friendship.' "

CHAPTER SIX

Berlin: Business Dinner

Galinsky and the Major got into a taxi on Alexanderplatz.
Sheets of rain mixed with snow slowed their progress toward the western section of the city. They stopped at
Candy, a good Charlottenburg restaurant. They went inside. The maître d' came over to greet them.

"Good evening, Herr Direktor. Would you like an
apéritif? The usual?"

"Of course. Make yourself comfortable, Galinsky.
They make the best martinis in Berlin here."

Galinsky nodded in agreement. He waited for the
maître d' to move away before asking, "Are you a regular
customer here?"

"I make a habit of eating here now and then. And
Direktor is accurate. I run a real estate agency. The office
is just around the corner."

A waiter brought the martinis. They drank. The Major offered Galinsky a cigarette.

"How are you feeling, Galinsky?"

"Now, I'm feeling fine. Until yesterday I kept thinking of a military psychologist who said lack of desire was a symptom of post-traumatic stress. I had the symptoms, without ever having seen combat. Odd, no?"

"Did you have any plans?"

"None. Whenever I tried to think, I was overwhelmed, crushed, by my situation. The farthest I got was buying one of those magazines for mercenaries, but I never opened it. I won't deny I'm still frightened about the results of my investigation. The waiting is unbearable."

"You have no reason to fear. We intelligence officers are untouchable. There's too much dirt involved, and it could splatter onto a lot of people, so no one would dream of stirring it up. The only ones in big trouble are civilians, the informers who collaborated with the Stasi, the poor saps who ratted on their neighbors. This witch hunt will go on for a long time, but it won't touch us."

"I like your optimism, Major."

"I know what I'm talking about. There's nothing to reproach in your past, Galinsky. You were in Cuba training Nicaraguan divers to deactivate depth charges. So what? The UN condemned the Americans for mining the ports. You were on a humanitarian mission and no one will blame you for it. You were also in Angola, training the same militia that subsequently protected Shell installations. In Mozambique you helped to protect the railway line and the Moputo airport. What is there to censure in any of this? Before that you taught Chileans and Bolivians how to use explosives. So what? They came from countries where mining is a major resource and they were introduced to you as workers with grants for specialized training. What you did with them comes under the heading of aid to development. You were a soldier and your every assignment had a basis in law. You simply obeyed the law."

The dinner was a sumptuous affair. The Major selected the wines with skill, and after dessert, while they were drinking an excellent cognac, he repeated that there was no cause to fear sanctions or reprisals.

"Of course someone has to expiate all the guilt. And this someone will be a senile old man who at this moment is packing his bags. They'll let him go to Chile, and there he will die in exile. The German sense of theater demands a tragic ending. Drink, Galinsky. To the health of our general secretary, president, last proletarian leader. The poor old man was such an idiot he wound up believing the homage he'd ordered them to pay him, the statistics and production figures he himself invented. Drink, Galinsky. You want to know what a bottle of cognac costs? As much as we used to earn in a year, you and I. But those days are over. Those lousy days are just a bad memory. A new day has dawned, and things are going our way."

"I'd like to see it that way too. Is there a recipe?"

"Indeed there is. The first step is to set yourself the only worthwhile goal: Get rich. The richer the better. Wealth is a blessing, poverty is obscene. Think about it, Galinsky. When the wall came down, we thought the people in the West, the Wessis, would view our poverty with pity, with compassion. And what happened instead? It disgusted them, they were repelled. Official speeches decreed that we were all equal, but we know that's not true. When one of us, a mangy Ossi, checks the time on his watch, his crappy Russian watch, he senses that time played a dirty trick on him, that time is rushing past him, that it's moving so fast he can't keep up. But when a Wessi checks the time on a bejeweled Rolex, it assures him that time belongs to him, that he's in charge. You've got to make up your mind to be rich, Galinsky, and men like you and me have everything it takes to get there. We were communists, so we know the rules of capitalism. And we were soldiers, which is to say, men trained to overcome defeat."

"Forgive me, Major. I don't understand."

"What inspires a soldier to act?"

"Everything that comes into my head sounds dumb to me."

"And probably is. You're young, Galinsky. You were always considered an honest officer, because you believed everything you were told. But I'm a veteran and I can tell you the truth: every soldier's raison d'être is, quite simply, the spoils of war."

They had another glass of that delicious cognac and left the restaurant. They strolled through the streets of Charlottenburg. Galinsky was aware of a sour aftertaste threatening to spoil his pleasure in the meal. Was this why the Major had made a dinner date? So that he could philosophize in a language of strange moralizing codes? To show him he could belong to the winning side too, but without going into helpful details? They came to the gates of a private parking garage and stopped.

"Open Sesame," said the Major, inserting his magnetic card into the automatic door.

They entered an underground garage. They passed two rows of cars and came to a Mercedes convertible. The Major used a remote-control switch to undo the safety locks on the doors.

"Like it? It's my favorite toy."

"It's yours?"

"Would you mind driving? I'm a bit tired."

They left the garage. Galinsky couldn't believe it. He was driving a car like in the movies. A Mercedes sports car. The dials on the instrument panel sparkled, and the city lights were reflected in the hood. Following the Major's instructions, he drove back to the eastern section of the city, feebly illuminated and lined with buildings as gray and stolid as the socialism they represented.

"Go down Unter den Linden. How do you say that in Spanish?"

"Bajo los Tilos. Avenida Bajo los Tilos. Where are we going, Major?"

"Are you in good shape, Galinsky?"

"In what sense, Major?"

"In the best sense. I have a mission for you."

"You give the orders. I told you yesterday."

"Like the old days. Only this time, instead of a tin-pot medal waiting for you if you succeed, you'll make a quarter of a million marks."

"I never felt better in my life. Order away, Major."

"Great. Stay on Unter den Linden. We're going to get laid."

The linden trees that give the avenue its name looked as musty as the surrounding buildings. As they passed the mausoleum for victims of fascism and militarism, the Major burst out laughing.

"They're selling everything off, Galinsky. How many times were you assigned to the honor guard at the mausoleum? Chilblains, the fatherland gave us. It won't be long before they sell it. I'll bet they'll open a hamburger joint on the site. They can do the french fries on the eternal flame."

They parked near Akademieplatz. Galinsky looked at the dimly lit facade of the Hotel Charlottenhof. The Major laughed again.

"Good old Charlottenhof. It must bring back memories of when you came to fetch the Latin Americans to take them to the Cottbus base. Whoever buys this hotel will find a fortune in wiring and hidden microphones. The Stasi used to install a mike for every guest, and we put in others, the KGB, the CIA, the Arabs, the Cubans, the Angolans. There are more mikes than bricks. I hear a Brit just bought the elevator cages."

Galinsky joined in the Major's laughter, and although he laughed, he couldn't help recalling a certain morning in 1980. On that occasion he had gone to the Hotel Charlottenhof to interview a Nicaraguan woman. The woman had arrived in the GDR with a delegation of children who were incapable of playing, and not because they didn't feel like it. They had no hands. Shortly before the Sandinista victory, Anastasio Somoza's national guard chopped off the hands of twenty boys who had thrown stones during the Masaya uprising. Twelve of them survived and came to Berlin to be given prostheses so that they could play again. The boys greeted him by raising their right wrists in a horrible parody of the proletarian salute. Galinsky swallowed his saliva and said nothing. To bring up a subject like that would be throwing a bucket of dirty water on their jolly night out and the good times just beginning.

They pushed one of those broad old doors that gave onto a typical Berlin passageway. On either side were stairways leading to the right and left wings of the building.

Near the stairways the mailboxes and electric meters were lined up in rows. They went ahead till they reached the door leading to the inner courtyard. Galinsky knew this kind of building very well. In the inner courtyard, the *Innenhof*, he expected to find blocks of apartments with peeling walls and precariously hanging balconies, and, silhouetted behind some poorly lit window, an old man reading or poring over a postcard collection.

To Galinsky's surprise, the building on the inner courtyard was half hidden behind scaffolding, festooned with the advertising posters of West German construction firms. The entire second floor was lit up, and the entryway smelled of fresh paint. A voice greeted them the minute they came through the automatic doors.

"Good evening. What is your pleasure?"

"A drink, or several, in good company," the Major replied.

A well-muscled fellow ushered them into the apartment. He recognized the Major and apologized for the strong smell of paint. He showed them at once to a spacious room. A group of women leaned on the American-style bar, chatting with the customers. They ordered gins.

"Of all the brothels that have opened, this one is the best. Cheer up, Galinsky. You have nothing to envy them on the other side. The owner is a guy from Munich who spent a fortune restoring the building. How do you like the girls? There's something for every taste. Look. With that dark-skinned one, you could practice your Spanish. She's Cuban. But where is my geisha hiding?"

At three in the morning, a heavy layer of snow covered the streets of Berlin. Galinsky went over to a window and opened it to breathe in the cold, revivifying air. He'd spent two hours studying the papers the Major had given him.

"Tired, Galinsky?" he inquired from the other side of the desk.

"No, Major. Impressed by the story."

"Good. You have two days to prepare your trip."

"Chile. I was never in that country."

"It can't be very different from Cuba. We'll celebrate your return in the same brothel. You can invite me."

"It will be a pleasure, Major. A real pleasure," said Galinsky as he returned the general catalog of the Zurich Numismatic Museum to the desk.

CHAPTER SEVEN

Hamburg: Time to Take Stock

I left Kramer at the entrance of the Lloyd's building and started walking, headed nowhere in particular. First I thought of going toward Zelma's Imbiss, then I wanted to stop by the Regina to pick up the money they owed me, but finally my distress won out, the need for four sheltering walls, and so I found myself heading upstairs to burrow in my den.

The downstairs neighbor must have been waiting for hours with his eye glued to the safety sight, or whatever they call those hateful vigilante peepholes. He waited till I had crossed the landing before opening his door.

"Listen. We want you to know that this is a respectable building," he spat out.

"We? I don't see the rest of the chorus."

"We've talked it over with the neighbors. The police

were here this morning searching your apartment. We're signing a petition. We want you out."

"Thanks for the warning. I appreciate friendly folks."

"Why don't you go back to Turkey?"

"Because I don't feel like it. Because I like to live surrounded by creeps like you. You understand?"

I stomped out the words on my way upstairs. The guy shut his door.

The apartment looked as if a hurricane had hit it. The books were scattered all over, the seat cushions had been slit open with a knife, and there wasn't much left of the bed either. In the bathroom sink a concoction of toothpaste, shampoo, and eau de cologne bubbled helplessly in the clogged sink. In the kitchen the open refrigerator illuminated a landscape of rice, soup packets, and suitably trampled noodles. On the living-room floor I found the victim of honor: Pedro de Valdivia's electric heater, with the wires cut. The cops had done a thorough job.

I removed the torn cushions from the sofa and fell onto the box spring. It was as cold inside as out. Apparently the heat was still off. I thought of the short guy in the blue ski cap. When I accepted Kramer's assignment, the cripple assured me Pedro de Valdivia would be freed without charges, but I couldn't help feeling I owed him an apology on several counts.

———

"Tomorrow you'll receive your tickets, final instructions, and an advance against expenses," Kramer had said when we parted.

"And a chance to play dirty with you. To mess you up."

"You won't do it. Although you refuse to admit it, you are beginning to realize what a good deal I've offered you. You are going to win, Belmonte. For the first time ever, you'll actually derive some benefit from one of your adventures."

"What do you know about winning or losing?"

"More than you think. And don't forget. You're working for me, exclusively."

I was going back to Chile. I lived in dread of that moment, not because I no longer liked my country—it was still wired into my nerves—but because I had always been immune to amnesia, especially an amnesia imposed for reasons of state, after political bargaining, by some crummy law.

What was waiting for me in Chile? Terrible fear and uncertainty. How would my stomach react, to give an appetizing name to the place where our soul is lodged.

And you are there, too, Verónica, my love, in your refuge made of silence, which I do not wish to approach, because I know you won't let me in.

From my reptilian vantage point, I suddenly spotted

my copy of *Journey to the End of the Night*, with its spine ripped off. Inside this book I kept the only letter that had ever shown me how much pain good news can conceal. I got up and searched between its pages. The letter was still there, folded up small, as if it too were feeling the intense cold.

Santiago, Chile, September 3, 1982

Señor Juan Belmonte,

You do not know me. My name is Ana Lagos de Sánchez and I am the wife of a disappeared prisoner. My husband, Angel Sánchez, was arrested on May 22, 1974, at ten A.M. as he was leaving the house to go to the hardware store for supplies. He was forty years old, and a plumber by trade. A number of people saw him taken away in a car without license plates and since that day I have had no news of him. Angel was a Communist Party militant. I am still one myself. While searching for my husband I began to take an active part in the work of the Committee of Families of the Disappeared. As you must know, we have managed to locate the hidden graves of many of the missing. Sometimes, all too rarely, alas, we have found some of our people alive, children for the most part.

One of the ways we conduct our searches is to leave the house early, right after curfew is lifted, to scour the garbage dumps and vacant lots on the outskirts of Santiago. We do this every day. I do not want to cause you distress, but I think we have found your companion, alive.

On June 19, 1979, a young woman turned up in a San Bernardo garbage dump. We were informed and went there. What I'm going to say now is very difficult, Juan, but I know you are a brave man. You were not in Chile. Your companion's father, a widower, searched for her actively until his strength gave out. Don Andres Tapia died in September 1978. He had managed to have Verónica Tapia Marquez declared missing by the Chilean courts. Our committee has photos of nearly all the disappeared; we were able to identify her from one of these photos.

Physically she is all right, Juan, but they destroyed her mind. She doesn't speak. Since we found her we haven't been able to get her to say a single word. Who knows what horrors she suffered and witnessed while the soldiers had her at their mercy.

Once we had identified her we began to look for her family, but as you know, Verónica's father was her only relative. She is living with me. For our mutual protection, I have told people she is my niece. She has been living with me for three years, and although she doesn't speak, and has remained withdrawn all this time, I have learned to love her like a daughter.

But at last I have found you. A few weeks ago, while we were waiting for the bus to go home after seeing a doctor friend who takes care of Verónica, a man came up to us who recognized her. She did not come out of her silence, so I asked this unknown person if by chance he was a friend of Verónica's and if he could help us to find other people who had known her previously. The man was scared. You could tell. There are so many cowards in this country. I insisted, and he briefly referred to you. He knew you had gone into exile.

After that I sought information from the Committee of Families of the Disappeared. As misery seeks company, we are, fortunately, in touch with the Mothers of Plaza de Mayo. We obtained your address from them.

I know that you neither can nor should return to Chile while the dictatorship lasts. I want you to know that Veronica is well cared for and that, although she doesn't know where she is—a prisoner, perhaps, of the horror she suffered—she lacks neither the affection nor the solidarity of the defeated who still believe in love.

I enclose my address and phone number.

I embrace you and hope your joy in knowing she's alive will see you through this painful moment.

Ana Lagos de Sánchez

And so Verónica returned, so you were returned to me, love, in photographs kind Señora Ana sent me later on. Your same childlike face, your eyes staring vacantly into empty space. Your long hair, streaked with gray. I nearly wore out the photo running my fingers over it, as I resolved, time and again, to live for you alone, for your well-being. I renounced the temptation to join the struggle in the jungles of Guatemala or El Salvador. I meant to live for you, so that you would lack for nothing, Verónica, my love. I would work at the lowest sort of job. I was ashamed that on that same nineteenth of July 1979, when you appeared, when you returned from the dead in a Santiago garbage dump, I was in Managua, laughing. How I hated these hands of mine, that touched the red and black sky on that day of the Sandinista victory. I was ready to return home at once, and how I despised myself when I realized that I longed to return not for you as you are now, lost in dreams, but to avenge the death of the woman you once were. And now I'm going home, Verónica, my love, and I'm frightened, very frightened, because that desire for vengeance shapes and guides my every waking thought.

Someone knocked at the door. I clenched my fists. If it was one of those neighbors, so prone to giving advice, I would send him back downstairs spitting teeth along the way.

Pedro de Valdivia looked at me with his one open eye. The other was swollen shut, and embellished with a purple hematoma.

"The cops made a mess, boss. They broke everything," were his first words.

"So I noticed. Come in."

"I told them you weren't here but they didn't believe me."

"That's what they're like. Incredulous. Who shut that eye for you?"

"It wasn't their doing. They stuck me in a cell with a drunken Norwegian who insisted on making me do a rain dance. But he got his, boss. I gave him a knock on the head that will keep him quiet for a few days."

Shorty took stock of the damage and shook his head. When he saw the electric heater with its works torn out, he frowned like an irate Cyclops.

"The bastards. The lousy bastards. They got the heater."

"Don't worry. I'll pay for it."

"That's not why I mentioned it, boss. The whole building has heat, except you," he said, and began to pick up books and other items from the floor.

While Pedro de Valdivia was hard at work restoring order after the police riot, I went to the kitchen to see if the forces of order had spared a bottle of something or other. I was in luck. They'd left a bottle of Tequila Cuervo thrown in with some cleaning supplies.

"Let it be. Let's have a drink."

"Pisco? I can run down and get some limes and make you a pisco sour."

"This is tequila. What real men drink. *Salud.*"

"This Mexican pisco is great," Shorty said, winking with his good eye.

By two P.M. Pedro de Valdivia had the apartment so neat it looked like a gang of housewives had gone over it. I helped him halfheartedly, but I was glad to have him around. The last bits of foam from the disemboweled cushions disappeared with the last drop of tequila.

"I'll come by tomorrow with needle and thread and have those cushions like new, boss."

"You're not going to ask what the cops wanted?"

"The cops always want trouble."

"They put you in the slammer because of me."

"A couple of hours. Does a fish mind water? What surprises me is that they let me go after I busted that Norwegian's face."

"You know something, Pedro de Valdivia? We're going out to eat at a place run by some Turkish friends."

"Terrific, boss. Are we celebrating something?"

"Why not? We'll celebrate my return to Chile."

On the way to Zelma's Imbiss, it started snowing. Shorty pulled his ski mask down over his face. Every other step he turned his head to look at me. The gleam in his good eye seemed to say that we were getting mixed up in something big, the sort of undertaking where the hardships would be unbearable without the company of a good comrade.

Interlude

I left my native Tangiers on the 13th of June in the
year 1325 (by the Christian calendar). I was twenty-
one years old and justified my decision with the ar-
guments of a pilgrim. Thus I left my parents, brothers,
wives, sons, friends, and possessions. I departed with
the solemn tranquillity of a bird abandoning the nest.
Only the Highest, the Merciful, the Worthy of Ninety-
nine Virtues knew in which direction I would be driven
by the winds . . .

(These are the opening words of the narrative that
Sheik Abu Abdallati Muhammad Ibn Abdallah Ibn
Muhammad Ibn Ibrahin Al Klawatti, known as Ibn
Batuta, along the seventy-five thousand miles that passed
beneath his foot soles, dictated over six hundred years ago.)

. . . During my travels, which are not yet ended—only the Unfathomable knows what I seek and whether I shall find it one day—I met three classes of voyagers: first, the devout pilgrims. May the Magnanimous watch over them. Then, the serene merchants who follow the tracks of the caravans. May the Perfect One guard and multiply their possessions. And finally, there are those who sigh as they contemplate the indefinable horizon of the sea. Strange men, with no attachment to the possessions Allah bestows on them. They would rather depend on his will during horrific storms, than enjoy the loving hospitality of the bazaar. Their souls find greater repose in the frightful roaring of the wind, than in the devout voice of the imam announcing the hour of prayer from the top of the minaret. May the All-merciful relieve their suffering, and mine, because these I feel are my brothers . . .

(In 1367, after he had roamed three continents for over forty years and blazed innumerable trails, Ibn Batuta sought refuge at the court of the sultan of Fez. In this city, where the wheel is banned, he was a guest at the honorable University of Quarawiyin. Assisted by the Andalusian poet Ibn Juzai, he gave two years to the task of editing his *Rhila*, a surprising book of journeys and sea voyages. The manuscript is now in the collections of the Bibliothèque Nationale in Paris.)

. . . The magnificence of Allah has preserved my memories and inspired the beautiful and cadenced words in which Ibn Juzai transcribes them. Life yet seems to me to be a great and sublime mystery, but it was not the will of the Unfathomable that I linger at the doors that guard his secrets, save for one. It was many years ago. I was enjoying the hospitality and homage of Muhammad Ibn Tuglug, sultan of India. May the Magnanimous maintain him in veneration, and humble his enemies. We were in the hall of the ninety-nine columns, in the palace of Yahanpanah, observing the meticulous work of some craftsmen. The men were covering the inside of a cupola with very small tiles. They began at the sides and slowly, the perfectly aligned pieces advanced toward the center, until there was left the minimum space exactly, for one last tile. Then the craftsmen interrupted their work in order to praise the perfection of Allah. There I understood that no traveler, no matter how far he ventures, is orphaned from the protection of the Highest, from his all-seeing gaze and his all-preserving memory. Pilgrims who never returned home, merchants whose caravans were swallowed by the torrid desert, sailors who lost the sea's horizon, those without graves watered by the plaintive wailing of widows, are also pieces of a mosaic created by the will of Allah, carried willingly by his unerring hand in search of the suitable place, the exact position.

Many of them will have found the eternal symmetry in lands that no other man is destined to visit, since the magnificent has so disposed. Others, like myself, unworthy of perfection, have not found their correct placement, but one day his infinite generosity will re-unite the scattered parts. Then the mosaic will be complete and afflicted souls will rest in the order of the Generous, the Devout, the one who is full of Mercy and Virtues . . .

(Ibn Batuta died in Fez, in 1369, at the age of sixty-four. His disconsolate protector, the sultan, ordered minted in his honor one hundred gold coins weighing ten ounces each, which were to be buried at one hundred different crossroads where the wayfarer had passed. But the sultan's will was never fully carried out, and the coins changed owners countless times. According to a note in the catalog of the Zurich Numismatic Museum, the last owner of the coins—sixty-three of the original hundred—was a prestigious Bremen silversmith by the name of Isaac Rosenberg, who died at the Bergen-Belsen concentration camp in 1943. The coins were last seen in Berlin in 1941. They are known as the Collection of the Wandering Crescent.)

Part Two

Living intensely makes every effort and every sacrifice worthwhile. Living halfway has always been the function and the punishment of mediocre people.

ROLO DIEZ,
A Tombstone in the Valley of Death

CHAPTER ONE

Altitude Thirty Thousand Feet: The Musings of an Insomniac

After dinner they showed a decidedly soporific film and most of the passengers snored away under Lufthansa's blue blankets. I followed the Indiana Jones movie without putting on the earphones. I was waiting for it to be over, and for the contours of Europe and South America to reappear on the screen, with a lot of blue space in between. A line of dots indicated the plane's route. We were flying very close to some patches identified as the Cape Verde archipelago. I felt that every one of those dots was another link in the chain tying me to an adventure I didn't expect to come out of in one piece.

Two days before my departure, I had a last meeting with Kramer. It was one of those days when the sun shines to no effect, when nevertheless the streets of Hamburg fill with people thrilled to see proof that the old star is still burning.

He had told me to meet him at nine A.M., at the Botanical Garden, a big park that starts downtown and ends near the docks. When I arrived he was already there, enjoying a degrading spectacle and a stream of invective from an old woman, as furious as she was appalled, because the cripple's repulsive dog was sticking it to her little bitch.

"Old degenerate. Do something to make that beast let go of my puppy," she said, brandishing a shopping bag that unfortunately failed to connect with Kramer's head.

"My good woman, you can't curb their instincts," he replied with a cynical smile.

"Please, sir," the old woman begged me when I came up. I wanted to give the dog a good kick while he was moaning in ecstasy, but I was out of luck because just at that moment he uncoupled from the little bitch. With his little red prick still stiff as a board he parked himself on the ground and bared his teeth at me.

"Thank you. I know the Koran prohibits this kind of filth for you people," the old woman said, and went off with her insulted mascot.

"Don't mess in Stinker's business. I'm giving you good advice," Kramer said by way of a welcome.

"How many breeds has your little horror debased?"

"Let's go have breakfast. Stinker has earned himself a treat."

We sat at an outside table. Kramer too felt the need to kid himself, exclaiming that the sun warmed his bones.

He ordered two mugs of coffee with madeleines and a soy burger for the dog.

"Soybeans are a great sexual reconstitutive. The Chinese know a lot about these things."

"As far as I'm concerned, they can feed poison to your crummy dog."

"You and Stinker will learn to love one another. I am sure of it. Got the tickets?"

"You know very well I have them."

"I'm just trying to be friendly. Let's see. What is your mission?"

"I travel to Tierra del Fuego. I meet up with one Hans Hillermann and convince him to give back sixty-three gold pieces. All very simple, unless a guy they call the Major gets there first and Hillermann and the gold are no longer in existence."

"He's not there yet. He hasn't left Berlin. I wanted to talk to you about that, Belmonte. I hired a private detective and found the famous Major. He's a former intelligence officer in the GDR army. Now he runs a real estate agency."

"A former intelligence officer. Then there's someone en route. He could be on his way home by now."

"Possibly. In any case, it means you have to act fast. I know and understand that you love Verónica."

"Don't say her name, Kramer. I don't want to hear my companion's name in your filthy yap."

"Down, Stinker! All right, but don't shout, Belmonte. The dog gets upset. Listen: whatever has to do with your personal life, you'll attend to once your mission is accomplished. I changed the time of your flight from Santiago to Punta Arenas. You'll have two hours in the Santiago airport and then you'll proceed to the south. I've made all the arrangements. You pick up your ticket for travel within Chile at the Santiago airport. You're going to get there before the other guy, Belmonte. You're going to win this match. You've got to win it and you know why."

Did I ever. From the outset, Kramer tried to make it clear that he had power over me. He managed to get the cops to wipe out my last defenses, that whole damned infrastructure of guerrilla fables. He wanted me stranded in limbo, with all the other dropouts who have nowhere to go, and nothing left but their useless principles. The way things stood, he had me on a tight leash. My principles begin and end with Verónica. They wear her name. Everything I did and do was aimed at meeting her slightest need. I don't know if Kramer underestimated my past. Maybe he thought he had me cornered in an alleyway and was guarding the lone exit from his wheelchair. Or maybe everything he did was meant to prove that guys like me think more clearly when we're thinking fast, when we're under pressure because things are closing in on us. Evaluate the situation on the move, we used to say in the old lingo, and that's just what I did as we strolled by the Elbe. He shoved me up against the ropes; that meant he needed me. He resorted to blackmail; hence we both had something to win or lose. And what's more, he mentioned a nice sum of money, as a reward for my services. In Nicaragua I learned something from Edén Pastora, one of the best guerrillas in history: a retreat under difficult conditions will work if disguised as a massive assault.

"All right, Kramer. I'll do what you ask, but there's a price."

"Let's hear it. Everything is negotiable."

"I don't give a crap about your money. I want something more: I'm going to carry out your mission, you'll get your damned coins, but you'll arrange to bring Verónica to Europe, to the best treatment center for psychological disorders."

"Agreed. The best Swiss clinic."

"No, Danish. In Copenhagen they have the best treatment center for torture victims. Regardless of the cost."

"I accept. As soon as I see the coins on my desk, I'll start to organize your companion's trip. Regardless of the cost."

The row of dots advanced slowly across the patch of blue, as if outlining a bridge between two shores. A stewardess asked me if I was having trouble sleeping and offered me a pair of dark glasses. I asked for a Jack Daniels with ice, and, glass in hand, I began to recall my departure from

Hamburg a mere eight hours before. It already seemed to belong to another life. I could barely manage to retain the details.

Pedro de Valdivia took me to the airport. Shorty was to stay put in my apartment. He had precise instructions.

"So, you know. If I'm not back in two weeks, you sell everything you can and send the money to the address I gave you."

"Don't worry, boss. You're going to come back. I don't know why you're going to Chile, but you'll be fine. I'm not asking any questions, boss."

"Of course. That's what I like best about you. February. It's summer there. I can't even remember heat."

"It depends, boss. In Santiago it's summer, but in the south autumn is on its way."

"Of course. I have an appointment in Tierra del Fuego."

"I'm from down there, boss. From Porvenir. You'd better take heavy clothing. This time of year is when the polar winds start blowing. I know what I'm talking about, boss."

"In other words, I'll never be free of my overcoat."

"An anorak would be better. Don't you have one? Never mind. I'll give you one of mine that's way too big on me. It's a down jacket."

The day I was due to leave he showed up with the green anorak. It was even big on me. We said good-bye with a handshake, and after I got past the police check, I looked back. Shorty was waiting, with a smile on his face and the ski mask pulled down to his eyebrows. One eye was still half shut.

After ten hours in the air it was a real pleasure to stretch my legs in São Paulo. The clammy heat clung to your clothes and your body. While drinking a cup of real coffee, at last, in the transit lounge, I suddenly had an alarming thought. What if that "someone," whoever it was, man or woman, the Major had sent, was traveling on the same flight? About two hundred passengers were traveling on our plane. I decided to pay attention to their faces. As soon as we were back in the air, I'd go up and down the aisles memorizing physiognomies. Another cup of coffee and it seemed like wasted effort. I was behaving as if I were a private detective, assuming that's the way freelance sleuths behave.

I knew the names of dozens of private detectives who solved cases in the murky world of mystery novels, but I had met only one flesh-and-blood detective, and his name I disciplined myself to forget.

It was in 1977, I think. The world was a kind of supermarket where revolutionaries of every stripe were stocking up on money and arms. I was returning to Panama from Mozambique, with two days to rest in Rabat. There I was supposed to meet up with a militant from the Polisario Front who was to give me a message for Hugo Spadafora. We arranged to meet in a café. From the moment we met, I liked the guy. His name was Salem, like the cigarettes, and he spoke a ceremonious Saharan Spanish.

"People have forgotten about us. Wars of national liberation aren't a salable item these days," Salem said.

"I haven't forgotten. I don't know much about the Saharans but I have a lot of sympathy for them. It must be because I always loved stories about the Tuaregs."

"Would you do something for us?"

"I'm delivering a message for Hugo. Isn't that enough?"

"This is something else. It involves retrieving a kind of plastic explosive we need. There's an arms dealer who double-crossed us. He gave us pure junk. That's no way to treat the sons of the desert."

"And where does this gentleman do business?"

"In Mexico City, which as you know is a quiet town, but he pushes his plastic in Luxembourg. We have his assistant there under twenty-four-hour surveillance."

From Rabat I traveled on to Panama and from there to Havana, to look for the man who would help me lend a hand to the sons of the desert. I don't know much about Mexico City, which figures, since no one can claim to know the biggest city on the planet. I knew even less about

Mexicans. A strange people, the Mexicans. Their history was without that traumatic rending signaled, in the southern cone, by military coups. They lived the lives allotted to them, they had a hard time of it, but they persevered stubbornly in the struggle for a better tomorrow. Unlike other Latin Americans, they didn't gamble away their chance for happiness in exchange for a bad check—the prospect of seizing power.

In those days I didn't know much about the Mexicans of Mexico, but I knew a lot about the Mexicans in Cuba. The year before I had become friends with Marcos Salazar, a professor who threw himself into the armed struggle in the late sixties, in order to complete Zapata and Villa's unfinished epic. They called themselves the Lucio Cabañas Movement, and at a time when the continent was shaken by insurrection, they saw their campaign as an integral part of the picture. They miscalculated. Cuba gave them no support. Revolutionary Cuba couldn't afford a blot on its relations with Mexico. Realpolitik. Conclusions based on an objective analysis of the correlation of forces.

They didn't last long. The Institutional Revolutionary Party unleashed a wave of repression and a group of militants, Salazar among them, hijacked a plane, in order to escape certain death. They flew to Cuba, and there they remained forever, or until the dreary spiderweb of history should dispose of their lives, deaths, fears, or other hallucinations.

I decided to take a stroll along the Malecón, a well-known Havana meeting place. Here I could pick up the thread that would lead me to Marcos. I bought a copy of *Granma* and read it through, sitting in a spot that was visible from all four points of the compass. I smoked nearly a pack of cigarettes, and watched the beautiful women of Havana go by, until at last I heard a familiar voice.

"What are you doing here, Belmonte?" It was Braulio, a dark-skinned man with a swinging gait. He was carrying a suitcase tied with rope.

"How are you doing, Braulio? Going on a trip?"

"Of course. I'm going to Switzerland to deposit the day's earnings. I am the exclusive agent, distributor, and salesman for an amazing product. Yes, gentlemen, upon my word, simply amazing."

"And who is the producer?"

"A tree. I'm selling avocados, dummy."

Braulio was one of those ingenious Cubans who live by their wits. A Bay of Pigs combat veteran since fallen into disgrace. But he never lost his sense of humor.

"I need to find a friend. A Mexican."

"That might be difficult. The head of PEMEX was here on a visit a week ago and they moved the boys out to Camagüey."

"Ten dollars could open a few mouths."

"Lovely words. You could be a poet. Come back tomorrow for another look at our fair Havana crops. Want an avocado?"

Marcos Salazar. I wonder what became of him. At that time he was in his forties, a tired-looking chain smoker. With that striking, tanned bald pate that made him look like anything but a guerrilla. A guy with the face of a lawyer, in a khaki jacket, trailed after him, pretending to stare at the waves.

"Belmonte, for God's sake. I can't believe my own eyes."

"How about a few *mojitos?*"

"I invite, the gentleman pays. Say, how do you like my guardian angel?"

"I already noticed. Are there any more?"

"No. I'm so insignificant they haven't changed him for months. The lousy snoop has practically gone cross-eyed ... you know what I'm saying? Never mind, bro, just spit it out as we're walking. Then we'll make with the rum and remembrance."

"I need a man in Mexico City. Someone who can beat the devil at his own game."

"I understand. Now pay attention: his name, you already forgot it, but you'll meet him in Azcapotzalco. The Lighthouse at the End of the World. He's missing an eye, I don't know which. Last time I saw him he had both."

"What do I owe you?"

"A binge that will last me for days."

Azcapotzalco was what in many cities is known as a sub-
urb. It didn't attach itself, like a boil, to the capital torn
from its Aztec mother. It was there first, waiting in am-
bush. Everything seemed to revolve around a gigantic
refinery that polluted the air. It took me only a couple of
questions to locate the Lighthouse at the End of the
World, a tavern where refinery workers and other members
of the brethren of the bar hung out.

"What'll it be?" the barkeeper asked.

"A beer. Listen, I'm looking for my buddy. He's a
client of the house. The guy who's missing an eye."

"And you think he wants to be found?"

"Sure. I told you, he's my buddy. And it's urgent."

"Just hold on. Who shall I say is calling?" the barkeeper reached for the phone.

"Robinson Crusoe."

I waited long enough to down five beers, in three gulps
each, sufficient time to become convinced that the world
was divided into motherfuckers and lousy bastards. I was
trying to decide which faction I felt more at home with,
when I saw the waiter craning his neck and sliding his lips
sideways to signal that my man had just come in. This
was a guy of indeterminate age, wearing a baseball cap and
a brown leather patch over his right eye.

"You're not Robinson Crusoe," he said by way of greeting.

"No, but I'm a friend of Marcos. He gave me your name on the island."

"Lousy Cubans. Hey, bro, bring me one of those misnomers."

"What's that?" the barkeeper asked.

"A Cuba libre."

The barkeeper filled his order. I watched how the one-eyed man stuck a finger in his glass to keep the lemon slice and the ice from falling out, while he got rid of the rum. He poured out the last drop and then filled the glass with Coca-Cola.

"It's called a kiddie Cuba libre. OK. Now what's this all about?"

I let him have the information Salem had given me. The one-eyed man listened, sipping his kiddie Cuba libre. I could tell from the way his eye blinked that he was already planning his moves. When I finished, he told me he wanted to see our objective.

The one-eyed man, whose name I forgot, drove a Volkswagen bug. We went clear across town—Mexico City seems to go on forever—till we came to a neighborhood of Hollywood-style bungalows. He parked fifty yards up from the house that concerned us, and trained his good eye attentively on the rearview mirror.

"It doesn't look difficult," he opined.

"I'd like to check out the area, make an operational survey."

"Now you sound just like a Chilean. I'll take care of all that. You're too easy to spot."

"Shall we talk about the risk factor?"

"What for? Robinson Crusoe is like a brother to me, and my brother's friends, et cetera."

He dropped me at a taxi stand. As we were saying good-bye, he gave me a card with instructions to phone him at eight P.M. On the card I read his name. Underneath, it said "Private Investigator."

I called him that evening as agreed. Strange people, these Mexicans. When they say yes, that's final.

"We're on for tomorrow. I'll stop by the hotel for you at oh six hundred, as General Patton used to say."

"All right. I suppose you have a tool for me."

"What's your lucky number?"

"Nine long."

That night I phoned Rabat and told Salem how things were going. The son of the desert informed me that on his end everything was progressing as planned.

The next day, shortly after daybreak, near a Hollywood-style bungalow in Mexico City, three men in yellow coveralls and safety helmets waited until a car with three people inside drove away from the house. Then they got out of their van. The one-eyed man was one of them; the second was a nimble youngster; I was the third. The one-eyed man addressed the youngster as Neighbor.

Neighbor didn't ring the doorbell, he leaned into it until a triple-wide refrigerator came trotting to the door. The pearl handle of a .45 stuck out of his belt.

"What's going on?" Refrigerator asked.

"Open the damn door so we can find the gas leak and hurry up because if we don't find it in time there's going to be a monster explosion and half the city will blow so come on let us in right now."

Refrigerator fell for it. A speech without commas never fails. We went inside. Neighbor kept sounding the alarm till a couple of other bodyguards showed up with sleep in their eyes, and a pair of housemaids.

"The leak is in this house and it's worse than we thought," Neighbor shouted, taking readings on an ammeter he wielded like a Geiger counter.

We went rushing into the bungalow and when we saw that the three goons and the maids were inside too, we took out our tools. One-eye was handling a black .45, Neighbor a snub-nosed .38, and I felt fairly safe with a nine-millimeter Browning.

"This band of creeps and the maids are for you, Neighbor. We'll go see the old man," One-Eye ordered, and we started kicking doors open.

Wolfgang Obermeier, alias Ernest Schmidt, alias Caesar Braun, former SS commander in any case, was sitting up in bed, eating a grapefruit with a spoon.

One-Eye stood in the bedroom doorway. His lone eye went back and forth between the hallway and the room. I jumped onto the old Nazi's bed and replaced his spoon with the barrel of my gun. Obermeier began to tremble. His eyes were popping out of his head. He drooled on the barrel of my Browning, with no regard whatsoever for Belgian industry.

"Listen up, old swine. You're going to see a photo of a man who's dying to know your address."

I took the photo out of my pocket. It showed a man in an Israeli army uniform. He was pointing to the numbers burnt into his arm. The old Nazi took one look at the photo and was ready to shit in his pants, just as Salem had predicted. Still drooling, he spluttered something incomprehensible.

"Take the gun out of his mouth. Can't you see the bastard wants to talk?" the one-eyed detective advised me from the doorway.

Before removing the gun from his mouth, I grabbed him by what was left of his hair. The old Nazi was trembling like a puppy dog.

"Who are you? What do you want?"

"Sons of the desert. But we're fond of those boys in the Mossad."

"My family . . . my family . . ." he stammered.

"I don't give a crap about your family. Now hear this: You are going to phone your agent in Luxembourg. You'll wake him up, but that's life."

Obermeier let himself be dragged to the desk.

"Keep the receiver uncovered. I want to hear too. And watch out what you say, because among my other talents I happen to speak German."

In a sweat, he dialed the Luxembourg number Salem had given me in Rabat. A few seconds passed, and then we heard a sleepy voice answer in German.

"It's me . . . Braun."

"Herr Braun? Is something wrong?"

I shoved the gun barrel into his free ear.

"Tell him to look out the window overlooking Marienplatz. Down below he'll see a bicyclist repairing his bike. Tell him to call the bicyclist and open the door for him."

Obermeier obeyed. The man on the other end began to ask questions, but the gun barrel crushing the old Nazi's ear helped him recover his old authoritative tone and he demanded obedience.

Three minutes later the man in Luxembourg informed him the bicyclist was upstairs. I spoke to him in Spanish.

"Greetings from Mexico."

"Greetings from the oasis," he replied.

I handed the phone back to Obermeier.

"Tell him to write a check in the amount of four hundred thousand dollars."

"But I got only half that much," he spluttered.

"What about interest?" said the one-eyed detective from the doorway.

With several millimeters of gun barrel poking into his ear, he gave the order to Luxembourg. A few minutes later I spoke again with the Tuareg.

"Got the cake?"

"Slathered in whipped cream. I'm going to go take a taste."

"Now, you bastard, tell your associate to see him to the door, to wait till he's gone and then return to the phone."

Five minutes later the man in Luxembourg was back on the line. He kept asking what else he should do.

"Tell him to pick up a book, any book."

The man in Luxembourg said he had *The Magic Mountain* on his table.

It was eight A.M. when he began to read Thomas Mann's novel over the phone. The one-eyed detective went to the room where Neighbor was guarding the three thugs and the two maids, and returned with them. It was a nice get-together and it lasted till one P.M. though the man in Luxembourg gave a very poor reading. At 1:05 I ordered Obermeier to hang up and phone Rabat. Salem sounded overjoyed.

"We cashed it. If you ever come through this way again, we'll celebrate."

"That's a promise, son of the desert."

Before leaving we made a solid bundle of the goons and the maids and left them in the cleaning closet.

Obermeier was trembling with fear and impotent rage. He dared to toss out one question while we were tying him to a chair.

"Are you going to hand me over to the Jews?"

"We play clean. I'd blow your brains out, but that would bring the cops down on us. And we won't hand you over to the Jews for one reason only: because you'd sell them everything you know about the Palestinians."

We left the bungalow and got into the van. Neighbor thought we'd made a nice haul of .45's. The one-eyed detective expressed concern over the phone bill we'd run up for the old Nazi.

Yes indeed. That one-eyed man was the only private detective I knew, and I thought how good it would have been to have him at my side in Chile.

No sooner had we taken off from Buenos Aires than I was overcome by fatigue. I could have sworn I had just settled down to spend the last hour of our flight pleasantly napping, when I felt someone's elbow in my ribs. I opened my eyes and saw the little fat man in the next seat.

"What's going on?" I asked, without knowing if I was awake.

"Look! Look!" Fatty answered, as if trying to jab a hole in the window with his finger.

"What?" I asked, half thinking we had an engine fire.

"The Andes mountain range. We're in Chile."

Blasted Fatty. He woke me up. I left my seat and edged my way up the aisle to the washroom. I looked at myself in the mirror. Hell, Belmonte, when you left Chile you didn't have a single white hair and now your head is divided into black and white, as if one part were a worn-out negative of what you used to be, and the other an even poorer copy of what you are now.

Santiago, Chile: A Saxon Nutcracker

The wooden nutcracker gazed at the room from the top shelf of the bookcase. In its outsize open mouth it displayed two rows of even white teeth. The upper row of teeth was painted on, beneath a thick purple lip. The bottom row was carved into one end of the handle, which served as a lower jaw. The handle ran clear through the body and came out in back, like a loose, low-slung hump. When you raised the handle, the mouth opened wide and the lower jaw dropped down to midchest on the doll. When you lowered the handle, the mouth clamped shut on the nut, or whatever else was inside, and crushed it.

The nutcracker was about a foot tall and made to resemble a haughty, disciplined Saxon lamplighter, of a type still in existence when Allied bombers buried Dresden in 1945. On its large, hydrocephalic head, it wore a black top hat. The body had been given a painted topcoat of blue, with gold buttons, epaulettes, and cuffs. White trousers with blue trim and black riding boots completed the outfit. In its right hand it held a long silver-tipped staff, and in its left hand, a six-sided lantern. Locks of horsehair stuck out from beneath the hat's narrow brim, and a pointy Wilhelm II mustache, painted in beneath the big nose, made the resemblance complete. The puppet looked useless and inert. Like any exile.

"Bigmouth came with me," said Javier Moreira, pointing to the nutcracker.

Moreira was a balding man in his forties, his hair as thin as his reasons for assuming a fake identity. He knew full well his interlocutor had his resume down pat. But the script was set in stone, and had its rules. Unconditional obedience to the rules was a mark of consistency. Javier Moreira was not his real name, nor was Werner Schroeders the name of the man seated across from him. Life, on the other hand, insisted on being itself: a farce.

"It's a museum piece. But they've started producing them in Hong Kong," Schroeders remarked.

"So it's all gone straight to hell."

"Some think just the opposite. They say it *was* hell; it didn't have to go anywhere."

"Gorbachev, that son of a bitch. They were too mild. We were all too mild, don't you think?"

"I'm a man of discipline. I don't think, I don't believe,

I neither form nor express opinions. I carry out orders."

Moreira went to the kitchen cupboard and started squeezing limes for pisco sours. He would have liked to find some grounds for optimism in the German's words. If an individual, a "cadre" like him, came to Chile to carry out orders, that meant someone was still giving orders. Perhaps the last battle had not yet been fought. But events had followed one another with such dizzying speed that reality weighed like a tombstone no ray of encouraging light could penetrate.

"Werner, were you expecting to find me?"

"I ran the risk, and I'm delighted to see I wasn't wrong."

Moreira bit his lips. He had been hoping for a "Yes, of course, comrade." He had returned to Chile in 1986, under terrible conditions. His party was falling apart, and his only move had been to rent a P.O. box at a neighborhood post office and make two copies of the key. One he sent to Cuba and the other to the German Democratic Republic. For nearly four years he showed up each Monday and Thursday, in disciplined fashion, to check the little cubbyhole embedded in a brick wall, and every time he found the emptiness that is the lot of the defeated, the shipwrecked forgotten on nameless islands, until one evening exactly seven days previous, the sight of an envelope dispatched from Berlin gave him an attack of tachycardia.

It contained an advertisement clipped from a German

magazine. "Mice? Give us your address and within a week we'll rid you of the infestation." The message was brief, but for Moreira it held more information than an encyclopedia.

"I'm happy to see you, Werner."

"I'll know that when I see how you perform."

Moreira served the drinks.

"Shall we drink a toast? To the good old days?"

"You're still a romantic, Moreira. I remember you as one of the few who got emotional over a toast to brotherhood between our peoples."

"In Rostock. With Crimean champagne."

"Or with rum. We had some real good times with the Cuban military attaché."

"To old times and noble comrades."

"You're hopeless, Moreira. To your health."

The two men had met in Cottbus in the early eighties. In those days there was considerable uneasiness at the Ministry of the Interior in the GDR, because the names of numerous Stasi informants had been leaked to the West. All the evidence indicated that the escape valve was of Latin American manufacture.

Werner Schroeders was an intelligence officer, known by that name in the Latin American section of the ministry. To him fell the task of finding a poison that would eliminate the worm at the very heart of the apple.

Javier Moreira's confidential file spoke of him as an unwearying communist. An outstanding activist with the Communist Youth organization. Military service with the naval infantry. Shortly after the '73 military coup he had joined the party's security apparatus. Until 1975 he worked underground, ensuring the safety of the Central Committee in Chile. From 1977 to 1979 he received military training in Bulgaria and Cuba. In late 1979 he was transferred to Nicaragua as one of those assigned to carry out ideological purges. His mission was to nullify the Trotskyist, anarchist, and Guevarist elements that had entered Nicaragua with the Simón Bolívar International Brigade.

"Who are you living with?" Schroeders asked.

"Why do you ask?"

"Your apartment has three rooms. That's a lot for a single man."

"You don't miss a trick. I live alone. When I returned to Chile, I got married but it didn't last long. My ex-wife took off with everything she owned, including the canary. You're safe here."

"The same thing happened to me. This is good stuff. Let's have another round."

Werner Schroeders watched him squeeze more limes. He read defeat in Moreira's movements. It was all too palpable, obscenely so. This was a far cry from the trustworthy man who, in an ancient East Berlin building in 1981, listened for hours without moving a muscle to the situational report being read to him, received his packet of forged papers, and took his leave, clicking his heels.

At that time Moreira proved himself to be an efficient worker, a "highly reliable cadre." He combed Frankfurt, Munich, Hamburg, Berlin, Leipzig, with the diligence of an ant. He went to countless Latino fiestas. He attended Masses, Catholic and Protestant. He listened to hundreds of records by Mercedes Sosa, Joan Baez, Inti Illimani, Pete Seeger, Quilapayún, Viglietti. He took part in protest marches for Bolivia, Chile, South Africa, Nicaragua, El Salvador, for all countries immersed in class conflict. He submitted to beatings at sit-ins in front of nuclear power plants and polluting factories. He danced with guys in gypsy drag at gay festivals. He smoked marijuana grown on balconies, and hashish purchased in Amsterdam. He fornicated in sleeping bags, in bourgeois king-sized beds, and in the great outdoors. In short, he led the normal life of a Latin American exile. Within six months, he found his way into the labyrinth and returned to Berlin with a composite portrait of the minotaur.

In the GDR the Stasi struck hard. The Germans implicated in the affair were brought up on charges of collaborating with the class enemy. Their property was confiscated and they were given long sentences in jails that had little or nothing to envy the dungeons of Pinochet or Videla. Those Latins who did not succeed in escaping were deported to their countries of origin, to the delight of dictators of all stripes. Then Moreira was ordered back to Frankfurt to close the case.

The brains of the courier operation was a Uruguayan militant who'd been part of the Tupamaro road show for many years. He watched the network fall apart, did some careful figuring, and uncovered the identity of the mole. Then he made a fairly objective analysis of the situation. The long arm of proletarian repression would not attempt to abduct him from Frankfurt. No. The sons of Papa Stalin were not that stupid. They would turn him over to the political police of the Federal Republic of Germany. He knew too much about the protest movement there. The West Germans would permit him to choose between serving as an informer or traveling home to Uruguay to rot in a prison with the paradoxical name of Liberty. This was a correct analysis. He was also correct in thinking he held a trump card: he knew Moreira's real identity. Chilean Communists and East Germans would not want to blow the cover of a man in whom they had invested their money, time, and trust. He saw a possibility for negotiation and made the first move, inviting Moreira to meet him in a public place. His proposal was simple and to the point: he would not reveal Moreira's identity or his role in thwarting the network. In exchange, he wanted to be left in peace for a couple of weeks, time enough to move to one of the Scandinavian countries, which he promised never to leave. He was ruminating all this when he saw Moreira appear at one of the entrances of the Konstablerwache subway station. What he failed to see, or to foresee, was the militant from the Kurdistan Workers Party, who shoved him onto the subway track.

"Tell me about yourself, Moreira. What are you up to?"

"I'm vegetating. I read, I take a crap, I sleep, and more of the same. I was on the losing side."

"The Party had resources."

"The Party. You know who was managing our finances in Berlin. A cadre. A big-time comrade, who studied in the Soviet Union and the German Democratic Republic. Now he has a trucking company and the one time I went to see him to ask for help he preached the gospel of the market economy. 'We can't create phantom jobs for workers, comrade. I understand your plight, but I'm not Catholic Charities, comrade. We were mistaken, comrade. And so, in all solidarity, comrade, you can starve to death for all I care. Now get out of my office before I call the police.' The Party. You want to know what I do for a living? I'm a butler, a custodian, but not to some lord. I'm the custodian at a nursery school. Every morning I have to clean, light the stove, check the swings to make sure none of the brats breaks his neck, polish the sled, repair dwarf-size tables and chairs, hang curtains, collect pacifiers and scissors left lying about. In the evening I pick up the shitty diapers. The Party. For two years I survived on the little bit of money I brought back from Germany, and later I lived on my ex-wife's earnings. Paying for the post office box, my contact with the cause, with men like you, Werner, sometimes meant living on bread and water for weeks. The Party. A few of our former leaders have good jobs, they're doing well. I once went to see one of them to ask for work, and do you know what he asked? 'What did you study, comrade?' My studies: geopolitics, historical and dialectical materialism, psychological warfare, sabotage techniques, counterintelligence, the theories of von Clausewitz and Ho Chi Minh, history of the Algerian resistance movement, tae kwon do. Rubbish. I'm not even fit to work as a garbage collector. The Party. It doesn't exist. It was all a farce, a miserable fraud. When the Russians pulled us off the tit in 1985, everything collapsed and it was every man for himself. And for the current leaders, guys like me are sorry adventurers. We're the ones responsible for the country's great misfortune. The debacle was all our fault. The Party. *Salud.*"

"That was an ugly speech, Moreira. I never thought the whole edifice would crumble the way it did. You had the fourth-best organized Communist Party in the world, after the Russians, the Chinese, and the Italians."

"It was all a sham. Shall I fix us another drink?"

"No. Do you still have it?"

"The rat-killer. Yes."

Moreira went to the bathroom. As he was removing the bolts that attached the mirror to the wall, he caught sight of himself and felt ashamed. He had carried on as if he were desperate, about to lose control. What good is a man in such a state? He was nothing but the dregs. He removed the mirror and with the aid of a crowbar dislodged the brick that sealed off his secret stash.

Before returning to the living room he rinsed his face. He placed the towel-wrapped package on the table and drew a deep breath. His self-confidence returned. He wasn't all washed up. Here was the proof.

Werner unwrapped the package.

"You think I could go back to Berlin?"

"A Colt nine millimeter, with a long barrel. An excellent gun. And what on earth is this piece of pipe?"

"A silencer. Chilean technology. We began to turn them out before '73. It's very simple. A steel pipe with ball bearings soldered inside, so as to form a spiral in the opposite direction from the gun-barrel grooves. It kills eighty percent of the bang. You attach it to the gun barrel from outside. It stays in place, but it's a good idea to hold it with one hand so the recoil doesn't knock it out of line."

"Terrific. Does it really work?"

"I never failed you. Werner. Answer me."

"Berlin. Don't even think of it. You haven't heard about the witch hunt they've unleashed? Someone would be sure to recognize you, and for the moment informing on others is the surest way to establish your democratic credentials."

"But there are comrades who could help me out."

"Forget them. They're ratting on one another. It's a way of surviving, and you surely know we Germans are champs at that. At the end of the Second World War everyone sold his neighbor for a chocolate bar or cigarettes. Now we do it for videos, cars, vacations in Torremolinos, a job."

"I can't believe it. There were thousands, hundreds of thousands of comrades. I saw them parade with raised fists, torches, the blue shirts of the Free German Youth. I was there. Anticommunism can't have taken over so easily."

"It no longer exists. Communism no longer exists, so no one can be an anticommunist. Now we're all anti-GDR. Don't you understand? Everything we did in the GDR was evil, perverse, rotten, shameful. For forty years we ate garbage, wore rags, fucked women with gonorrhea, and produced idiot children. But that's finished, and now, in exchange for a sincere denunciation, the West pardons us, redeems us, puts us in an air-conditioned womb, our umbilical cords are hooked up to a can of Coca-Cola, and then we're expelled through the birth canal of

Lady Mercedes Benz. Hallelujah, Moreira. We've been reborn."

"You can't be serious, Werner. Do you take me for an imbecile? You're trying to provoke me or test me. I'm not stupid. You're here for something, Werner. You must have had a reason to hold on to the post office box key. You've come to carry out a mission. And you need me. Like in the old days."

"That's right. Did you check it out?"

"It works perfectly. They still think highly of me, right?"

"You're our man across the Atlantic. Blindfold me, like in the old days."

Moreira obeyed, and to make sure the handkerchief was good and tight he made as if to punch Schroeders, stopping within inches of his blindfolded face. The German did not react.

"Take it apart, Moreira."

With precise gestures, Moreira removed the cartridge clip, released the safety catches, caught the recoil spring in the palm of his hand, detached the barrel from the firing mechanism. Within seconds the gun had been reduced to a puzzle, its pieces scattered.

"Ready, Werner. Begin."

"Time me, Moreira."

The German's hands moved like two automatons, quick and precise. Every finger had a job to do, holding or pushing the parts, and they kept moving until the gun had regained its final, lethal form, with a bullet in the firing chamber.

"Time."

"One minute and five seconds. Not bad, Werner."

"I'm getting old. I always managed it in under a minute. Let's see how you do."

"You have to give me a chance. This inactivity is driving me crazy. I never failed you all. You know that, Werner."

The German blindfolded him, checked in turn, to make sure he was unable to see, and stared at him fixedly.

"A military cadre can overcome any situation. That bit about going crazy doesn't sound very consistent, Moreira."

"I know. That's why I'm scared."

"I have something for you, Moreira. You're going on a long journey. No. Don't remove the blindfold. I want to make sure you're in shape."

"I knew it. As soon as I saw your note I knew you wouldn't abandon me. Mix up the pieces. I was always the best at this game."

But Frank Galinsky didn't dismantle the gun. He attached the silencer of Chilean manufacture and took aim at the blindfolded man's head.

The bullet struck Moreira between the eyes. He fell

backward, chair and all. On the floor, he managed to remove the handkerchief covering his eyes, but from his hu-
miliating vantage point the German at the other side of
the table was not visible. The last thing he saw was the
cynical grin on the face of the Saxon nutcracker.

CHAPTER THREE

Tierra del Fuego: Intimacies

The old man removed the bib of his greasy overalls and sat down on the bed to let Griselda help him out of the trouser part. Then he stretched out on the bed and studied the new corrugated tin ceiling, gleaming with reflected light from the flickering lamp. The woman asked him if he wanted to put on his nightshirt and the old man replied that he preferred to stay as he was, in his long johns and flannel shirt. His clothes were so grimy with sweat they had taken on the same ashen color as his skin. He lay his head back and let out a sigh. An unintelligible murmur rose from his throat, the sort of noise a man makes who's lived so long he can no longer distinguish between pleasure and pain.

"Are you feeling ill, Don Franz?" the woman asked.

"Just tired. And what's it to you, you old busybody?"

"That's what you get for being so stubborn. I don't know why you had to redo the roof at the end of the summer, and not let anyone help you. I still don't understand why you did it. The old thatch roof was much better. We're going to freeze in here, with that tin roof."

"Nonsense. Soon it will snow and everything will be nice and warm. The Eskimos live in ice houses. Do you know who the Eskimos are? How would you know, stupid old woman."

"You're crazy, like all gringos. And cover yourself up, your privates are showing."

"If you don't sew my buttons on, my prick slides out. It's not my fault. And if my prick bothers you, look at something else, you old hussy. What did you make to eat?"

"Chicken soup. You know you're not supposed to eat anything heavy at night. Dr. Aguirre said so."

"Bunch of crap. Dumb soups. What does that veterinarian know? I want something I can sink my teeth into, you understand? Outside there's a rib cut from the . . . how do you call that sheep with horns that Jacinto brought?"

"Goat, Don Franz. Goat. Jacinto brought a rib roast of goat. It's unbelievable how after so many years here you haven't learned to speak like a Christian."

"I speak Castilian better than you, you old scold. Make me a roast and put on some music. Lots of music."

"As you wish. I'll roast you a piece of that horned sheep, but don't complain later if you have a belly-ache."

From his bed, old Franz watched Griselda remove the embroidered cloth covering the Victrola. She raised the wooden lid and turned the crank. From a closet she took out a stack of old 78 records and selected the old man's favorite. The needle dropped into the groove and the room was filled at first with the sound of tiny voracious rodent teeth, gnawing a hole in time. Then a male voice filtered through, half melancholy, half jaded, singing a song that made you feel more like marching than whirling dizzily around a ballroom. Griselda couldn't understand a single word of what that man was singing, but she felt that this husky voice must arouse great passions in the old man's unimaginable homeland. Each time she heard it, she came to the conclusion it must be the voice of sailors on the high seas.

The old woman stoked the fire in the hearth. With a short-handled poker she separated two piles of glowing embers and shoved them under the grill. Then she went out into the clear autumn night. As always, she stopped to cross herself under the thousands of stars guarding the souls of the shipwrecked. She cut a generous portion from the goat carcass, which had been hung up to dry on a wire. She went back into the house, threw the meat on the grill, seasoned it with rock salt and dried rosemary twigs. From the bed the old man shouted orders. Make sure the fat gets good and brown, bring me a glass of wine, turn over the record.

Griselda finished grilling the meat and turned to look at the old man. His eyes were shut, in an expression of serene satisfaction she had never seen in him before.

"The roast is ready. Come to the table."

"Bring it. I'm going to eat in bed."

"You'll get the sheets dirty, Don Franz."

"Don't interfere with my bed and I won't interfere between your legs. Or would you like that, you overheated old woman?"

"Don't be crude, Don Franz. Or I'm going right now."

"I'm just kidding, old dunce. I don't trot anymore. My poor prick is only good for peeing and even there I have trouble at times. Serve the roast and drink wine with me, old biddy."

The old man ate with a healthy appetite. He devoured the golden ribs one after the other. Ignoring Griselda's disapproving glances, he wiped his greasy fingers on the sheets. He drank three glasses of wine, and then, apparently somewhat tipsy, ordered her to pour him another, and to turn over the record again.

Griselda obeyed. She turned the handle on the magneto, flipped the record, put a couple of logs on the fire. When she returned to the old man she found him humming the refrain of the song.

"Auf die Reeperbahn nachts um halb eins . . . Do you know who's singing, you old Patagonian?"

"How would I know that, Don Franz?"

"Hans Albers. He was like Carlos Gardel. Women wet their pants for him."

"And what does the song say, Don Franz?"

"It's about a street in Hamburg with more whores than there are sheep down here. Beautiful street. The most beautiful street."

"You're a strange one, Don Franz. And piggy. You'd better not drink any more wine."

"It's just a joke, old whiskerface. Have some wine yourself. We have to talk, but first, repeat to me what your son said."

"Again? I already told you twenty times."

"That doesn't matter. Repeat it, you old parrot."

Griselda smoothed her apron. She took a sip of wine and recounted once more how, at the Punta Arenas post office, where her son worked, a foreigner had come in asking where he could find Post Box Number 5 in Tierra del Fuego. And the foreigner had asked about someone named Hillaman, or Halmann, he wasn't sure.

"Hillermann, you old deaf-mute, Hillermann."

"Could be. Around here we have Christian names. Why are you so worried? The outlander didn't mention your name. My son told him he knew a lot of gringos, but none with that name."

"Turn over the record, you old crosspatch."

Griselda obeyed again. From the Victrola she went to the fireplace to put the kettle on the embers. While she was shaking the gourd to replace the maté with a fresh batch, she turned toward the bed. The old man lay on his back again, gazing at the shiny tin ceiling.

Those gringos are strange, Griselda thought. Look how he put a stable roof on his house. The old man held up his empty glass.

"Griselda, is it cold outside?"

"It's getting there. The Strait was dark blue and today I saw two bustards flying north."

"How many years have you known me, old dummy?"

"Twenty? More? I had just lost my husband when you came to repair the machinery at the sawmill. Twenty years, more or less."

"Listen, old dunce, and don't answer back. If I should die some day, all this, the house, the sheep, the plot, is yours. The notary in Porvenir knows about it. Dr. Aguirre knows too. It's all yours, so don't let anyone rob you, you old dimwit. The horse is for your son. You don't give the poor old nag enough hay. With you he'd die of hunger. All you give him is soup. Do you understand?"

"Don't say such things, Don Franz. It brings bad luck for the guanaco to give away his skin before the condor grabs him."

"Don't argue with me. All yours. But on one condition.

You must never sell or tear down the house. Or redo the roof. This house is my monument. When you die, you leave it to your son. He'll know what he's doing."

"You're scaring me, Don Franz. I hope you don't have dirty secrets, I hope you're not like Don Walter Rauff, that gentleman in Punta Arenas. A lot of people came and tried to kidnap him. People say they were Jews and they came in a submarine. Some people even got killed in that business."

"But they didn't grab him. Too bad."

The old man ordered the woman to turn the record over again. He lay back and lit his pipe, and smiled when he discovered the sharp flavor mingled with the aromatic Danish tobacco. He recognized Griselda's protective hand. When no one was looking, she tossed bits of horse turd into the tin. Like everyone in Patagonia and Tierra del Fuego, Griselda believed in the antirheumatic properties of horse turds. If she didn't put them into his tobacco, she put them in his maté.

The old man smoked his pipe and gazed intently at the objects that had kept him company for more than twenty years. Most of them, like the house itself, were the products of his own invention, his own skillful hands. The house was a spacious craft built from the remains of a Yankee clipper that had gone aground on Cape Cameron reefs. Fine solid wood from Oregon, with the joints nicely tarred, had gone into the walls. The planks of the deck, polished by the waves of the seven seas, made a warm floor for the 750 square feet of his house. The front door faced southeast, toward Useless Bay. The back door faced northwest, looking toward the Boquerón Heights. A dividing wall built of paneling from the unfortunate boat separated the pantry from the rest of the house. Within, a stone fireplace the height of a horse spoke of quiet snowbound winters. Behind the house a plank path, with a border of apple trees, led to the outhouse. It was one of the best houses in the area, and now crowned with a new roof of shiny tin. A smile flitted across the old man's face, as he sensed that he was beginning to take leave of his house without the slightest trace of regret.

"They can come any time, the bastards. They'll be right on top of what they're looking for but they won't succeed in finding it, because they only know how to look in sewers," he muttered in his old language. He noticed the old woman nodding off in her chair.

"Griselda?"

She made no reply. She was asleep, sitting up with her hands folded in her lap. Yes indeed. He had met her twenty year ago, or more. He remembered those days when, fed up with living like an old cormorant at the southern tip of Navarino Island, he decided he had been hiding for too long, and that the bothersome treasure stored in a brass box was getting to be just a boring joke played on him by an ironic destiny. So he moved to Tierra del Fuego, to work as a mechanic in a sawmill at Lago Vergara.

No one asked questions in Tierra del Fuego. Every outlander who arrives in this remote region is escaping from something, or from himself. In these latitudes the past does not exist.

He lived at the sawmill for several years, among fine men and fugitives from justice, until one day, crossing Useless Bay, he discovered the remains of the boat. The sturdy composition of its timbers was a sign to him that it was time to build his house.

Someone back then told him that solitude was ill regarded. They mentioned Griselda, Abel Echeverría's widow. A diver after shellfish he had been. One unlucky morning he descended into the mussel shoals of the Almirantazgo fjord, and returned to the surface three months later, thirty miles to the south, wrapped in half a ton of ice. Nilssen found him, an old man who roamed the southern seas in a cutter that was legendary, the *Finisterre*. Nilssen and his colleague, an Alakaluf Indian giant called Little Pedro, towed him back to Puerto Nuevo. Because it was winter, they buried him in the same coffin of ice in which they'd found him.

It took old Franz a good many years to wear down the widow's resistance, and when at last one brief summer night he finally managed to gain admission between her sheets, the two of them discovered that their lives were deeply steeped in memories best left unspoken, and that all they could do together was try to construct new memories, untainted by nostalgia. Such memories, if they can be achieved, offer the warmest sort of refuge. But since this takes time, they decided to live as gringo bachelor and part-time housekeeper, a relationship Griselda legitimized by invariably addressing Franz in formal terms.

"Griselda, you old seal."

"Yes, Don Franz. Forgive me. I seem to have fallen asleep."

"What a lie. You see my prick and you want to get in bed with me."

"You are impossible, Don Franz. I'd better go. Tomorrow I'll change the sheets; look how greasy you got them."

"Is it cold outside?"

"Yes. I already told you, the Strait has changed color. Any night now we'll have the first frost."

"Poor old buzzards."

"Buzzards? What buzzards?"

"The chimangos. When I went out to the road I saw two of them and while I was redoing the roof I saw some again. They must feel the cold up there."

"I'm leaving the kettle on and the maté all ready."

Before stepping outside, the woman pulled on a thick poncho and covered her head with a woolen cap. She tossed some more wood on the fire, said good night, and closed the door after her.

The old man heard the joyous barking of Griselda's dog. He got out of bed and went to the window. He wanted to watch her ride off on her docile dapple-gray mare, but all he could see was the reflection in the windowpane of his own tired face.

Hans Hillermann poured himself another glass of wine. He threw a jacket over his shoulders, dragged a chair to the fire, and sat down. From a jacket pocket he took out the letter he'd received a week before. He read it for the last time and threw it into the flames.

"They're here, Ulrich. Thanks for the warning. I don't know how many there are, but they're here. *Salud.* What a shame you'll never get a taste of Chilean wine, Ulrich. It's thick and dark like a German night. *Salud,* comrade. I waited for you for forty-some years. I could have melted down that shining filth and sold it by weight, but I waited for you. I was sure that one damn morning you would show up. How fine it would have been to sit and chat over a bottle of wine, by the Strait of Magellan, and throw our useless fortune into the sea. It was a lovely dream, Ulrich, just lovely, but obviously a cat can steal a steak from the butcher, but never a whole side of beef. *Salud,* Ulrich. I'm going to screw them in your name."

Hans Hillermann rose, went to the shelf where he kept his wine and tobacco, and took down his double-barreled shotgun and a couple of cartridges. Then he went to the

Victrola, cranked the magneto, and set the needle in the groove.

"Auf die Reeperbahn nachts um halb eins," he sang softly. And those were his last words, because at that precise moment his right thumb pressed both triggers. Hans Albers sang on alone, and the shiny tin ceiling was spattered with drops of blood.

CHAPTER FOUR

Santiago, Chile: Life Goes Round

The sun beat down on the Santiago airport at nine in the morning. Well, what do you know. Here I was with my feet on Chilean soil, after sixteen years out in the wide world. Why didn't you come away with me, Verónica? Why didn't some witch sell us a magic potion for predicting the future? Why did an obsession with that indefinable trait we called consistency have to interfere with our love, and keep us in different political factions? Why was I such an idiot?

"Belmonte, Juan Belmonte," said the Interpol agent, examining my passport.

"Yes, that's my name. Is something wrong?"

"Nothing. This is a democracy. Nothing's wrong."

"So?"

"It's just that you have the same name as a famous bullfighter. Did you know that?"

"No. This is the first I've heard of it."

"You ought to read about him. Belmonte was a great bullfighter. Say, it's years since you were last in Chile."

"That's how it is. I'm an addicted tourist and the world is full of interesting places."

"I'm not interested in what you did abroad or your reasons for leaving. All the same, I'll give you some free advice: this is not the same country it was when you left. Things have changed, for the better, so don't try to make trouble. This is a democracy and everyone is happy."

The guy was right. It was a democracy. He didn't even bother to say that they had restored democracy, or that democracy had been restored. No. Chile "was" a democracy, which was the equivalent of saying the country was on the right track and anyone asking awkward questions could dislodge it from the correct path.

Maybe this same guy had made his career, in part, in prisons that never existed, with addresses no one can remember, interrogating women, old people, adults, and children who were never arrested, with faces no one can remember, because when democracy spread her legs to let Chile inside, she named her price beforehand, and demanded payment in a currency called forgetting.

Maybe this same guy who now felt entitled to warn me not to make trouble was one of those who were brutal with Verónica, my love, with your body and your mind. And now he's enjoying the peace of mind that comes with winning, because they beat us, my love, they walked all over us, they won the Olympics. They didn't even leave us the consolation of believing we lost fighting for the best cause of all. And since you can't throttle the first suspicious son of a bitch you meet, I decided to move away fast from the police checkpoint.

I followed Kramer's instructions. As soon as I got past the checkpoint I went to the ticket window for domestic flights. They gave me the tickets for the rest of my trip to Punta Arenas. I had two hours to kill, so I left my suitcase and went outside to enjoy some hot weather.

The airport is surrounded by a park full of pine trees. I bought the first magazine that caught my eye and headed for a bench. Seated in a shady spot, I studied the course of the sun and turned to face the south. Somewhere in that direction was where Veronica lived. I was almost glad I had a ticket to Punta Arenas in my pocket. I was that anxious and fearful about a reunion.

I opened the magazine. The difficulties of the Chilean national soccer team, an increase in exports, delighted tourists spending the summer holidays at our seaside resorts were in the news. What stood out were the photos of people smiling triumphantly, as if the future belonged to them. Underneath their well-cut suits and designer ties, I recognized several former leaders of the revolutionary left. I didn't care about them. I'm still tough. I don't lose control right away just because something disgusts me, but I do believe I jumped when I saw the photo of a man with his eyes open and a hole in the middle of his forehead.

It was a crime report.

> Bonifacio Prado Cifuentes, forty-five, married, unemployed, was found dead in his apartment at Ureta Cox 120, apartment 3-C. Prado Cifuentes had been shot at close range. According to information provided by the Homicide Brigade, Prado Cifuentes had been dead for forty-eight hours when he was found by his wife, Marcia Sandoval, from whom he was separated. Neighbors in the building questioned by the police said they had heard no sound of fighting or of shooting in the apartment of the murder victim. Prado Cifuentes worked as custodian at the Firefly nursery school, in the San Miguel district. His colleagues at work described him as quiet and reserved.

Talk about life going round. I'd been wanting to meet up with that SOB for years. All I knew about him was his nom de guerre, Galo, Comandante Galo, and now, within half an hour of my arrival in Chile, a magazine delivered him to me with a hole between his eyes and his identity fully revealed.

I had met him under the worst possible circumstances, in Nicaragua in 1980.

We international soldiers of the Simón Bolívar Brigade
had heard about the arrival of a Chilean and Argentine
contingent, guys trained at military academies in Cuba, the
USSR, and other socialist countries. They showed up in
Nicaragua after the last shot had been fired against
Somoza's national guard, to carry out an ideological purge.
We weren't afraid of them; they didn't worry us. Maybe
we had been infected with the Nicaraguan mind-set, that
balls are what count. Guys who hadn't been around during
the shooting had no right to be in our group. But they
thought otherwise.

One January night in 1980 five masked men surrounded me near where I lived. I made a minimal attempt
to plead my case, to which they responded by hitting me
with the butts of their pristine unsullied Kalashnikov rifles,
which had never fired a shot against Somoza's national
guard. I remember I passed out while they were pounding
me into the floor of a jeep. When I opened my eyes again
I was lying naked and beaten to a pulp, in an empty room.
The stompings were repeated several times, with intermis-
sions as needed, to make sure I was never unconscious long
enough to enjoy it. Those gorillas were skilled workers.
They knew that by the time their victim came to after four
or five KOs, he'd have lost all notion of time and have no
idea where he was. But I knew that room perfectly well.
And then Galo turned up.

He had them seat me with my hands tied to the front

legs of a chair. Parrot's perch, bureaucratic style, we used to call that position in our old lingo. It wasn't the most comfortable posture, because you want to bend over, and the gorilla holding me up by my hair impeded that. Galo sat down next to me, with his face uncovered.

"Take a good look at me. I am Comandante Galo and we are going to have a long talk. Your name and nationality."

"Column Commander Ivan Leiva. Nicaraguan."

"I don't give a fuck about your rank. Your name is Juan Belmonte and you're Chilean."

"Column Commander Ivan Leiva. Nicaraguan. Your men have my papers."

"I wipe my ass with them. You're a Chilean; you've infiltrated in order to destabilize the revolutionary process. You're a CIA agent."

"You paranoid Communist. Prove it. And if you want to confuse me, tell your gorillas to take me somewhere else. I know this room. I know where we are. In the bunker. In this very room, we tried a number of spies after the victory. You do know what I'm talking about? There was an uprising in Nicaragua."

The stompings went on for two weeks. The accusations were downgraded. I went from CIA agent to provocateur, and then to Trotskyist, anarchist, and finally my great sin was to have fought with Chato Peredo in Bolivia.

I was into my third week in the bunker when luck brought a Sandinista comandante my way.

"Brother. What are you doing here, stark naked?"

"Ask Galo."

He got me out, cursing those thugs in fancy uniforms, the kind who clicked their heels and placed their fist over their heart when answering a question. We went for a long walk through the tumbledown streets of Managua and the Sandinista told me what Galo was doing.

"Our comrades in the Simón Bolívar Brigade got the full treatment. They took away their weapons, they arrested them. They put them on trial. Well, after their fashion. The Brigade no longer exists, brother. We're sorry, but politics is the art of the possible and the Cubans are making demands. You understand."

I understood. I understood so well that I had to give up my recently acquired Nicaraguan citizenship, and my new identity. I had to go back to being a Chilean, named Juan Belmonte. I had to leave Central America. But at least I lived to tell the tale. Others were less fortunate. They disappeared in the dungeons of Argentina, Paraguay, Uruguay, because Galo saw to it that they were returned to their countries of origin.

I was beginning to feel kindly toward Galo's assassin, when I picked up on a detail that started me worrying. Alongside the front-page photo of his face there was another, of the room where he was found. His body lay next to an overturned chair.

Near his feet you could see a bookcase, and on the top shelf stood an object with a familiar shape.

The details in the photo were fuzzy. I returned to the airport lounge and went straight to the newsstand. I was relieved to see they sold reading glasses. I bought a pair and with their help recognized the magnified image of the doll. It was a wooden nutcracker. A typical Saxon nutcracker.

I didn't like this at all. And whenever I don't like something, my brain cells start working overtime.

The magazine account said Galo had been working in a nursery school for the past two years. That meant he returned to Chile under the dictatorship. In 1980 he was a young guy gaining experience and racking up points. After his work in Nicaragua the Party must have moved him to a hard-line socialist country. Not to Cuba. We Latin Americans with accounts to settle always find each other sooner or later. The Colombians in the Simón Bolívar Brigade who managed to get out of Nicaragua unharmed had sworn vengeance. So Cuba was out. And China, and Korea. Our slant-eyed comrades did business with Pinochet. The USSR was out too. The Soviet Communist Party froze military training for Chileans in that very same year, 1980. The Soviets discovered that the dictatorship had infiltrated the military apparatus of the

Chilean Communist Party. So the USSR was out. Galo deserved a reward for his achievement in Nicaragua, and the only place he could receive it was Cottbus, at the military intelligence academy of the GDR. That Saxon nutcracker was forceful proof that Galo had been at Cottbus. It also raised many questions. If Galo spent time in Cottbus, did he meet the Major? Was he the Major's man in Chile? If all this turned out to be true, Galo's dead body presaged difficulties neither Kramer nor I had anticipated.

"I'd like to change my flight to Punta Arenas," I said to the girl at the airline desk.

"When would you like to travel, sir?"

"Tomorrow or the next day."

"I'll make the reservations, Señor Belmonte. But please, if you're not going to travel then, make your cancellation several hours before departure."

"Thank you, that's very kind of you."

"Don't mention it. This is a democracy."

Santiago. What an ugly city. The midday sun beat down like a punishment. I exited from the subway at Gran Avenida, a few yards from Ureta Cox street. I didn't know what I was looking for in Galo's apartment, but I was sure I would find it. There was a factory across the street from the building. Several workers in blue coveralls were gathered about a refreshment stand. I went up and asked for an ice cream.

"Shit, it's hot," said a short fellow who reminded me of Pedro de Valdivia.

"You said it. It's hotter 'n blazes," I replied, surprised to find my command of Chilean returning.

"And here I am working, like a jerk," the little guy added.

"Got to work."

"Sure do. And you? What's your grind?"

"I'm a bill collector for a furniture factory. I'm waiting for a customer who lives across the street."

"Over there, where they took that guy away?"

"Right there. Odd you don't see any police around."

"They're there. They left a couple of policemen, but they went for lunch at the bar on the corner."

I took the stairs two at a time. Three C wasn't locked, as if the plastic strip put in place by the precinct would serve as a barricade. I went inside. The first thing I saw was the outline of Galo's body, marked in chalk on the floor. I went right to the bookcase and took down the Saxon nutcracker. I turned it over. It had a dedication in German: "Genosse Moreira wir werden siegen. Berlin, 7 November 1985." Comrade Moreira, ours will be the victory. Did that boilerplate turn them on in the GDR? A memento for the anniversary of the Bolshevik Revolution. I went through the rooms, not knowing what I was looking for, until it struck me I was being dumb. Come on, Belmonte, I said to myself. Where would you hide your stash?

I wrapped my fist in a towel and broke the bathroom mirror. It wasn't hard to find the loose brick. In the stash, I found a cleaning rod for a nine-millimeter pistol, a can of Walter oil, and a key engraved CHILEAN POSTAL SERVICE 2722.

I walked out, calm as you please. Apparently, the police were enjoying a good lunch.

When I got to the corner of Gran Avenida and Ureta Cox it occurred to me that all I had to do was take the subway and in five minutes I would be at Señora Ana's house. Would Verónica react? Would it be, my love, as if you were waking from a long sleep? Would you ply me with questions? Would I find the courage to answer them? Key in hand, I entered a restaurant.

"What'll it be?" the waiter greeted me.

"The menu. What do you have?"

"Corn pie, salad, roast beef and french fries, wine or water."

"Roast beef."

"No. You get the whole meal, including dessert, of course."

I was surprised to realize I didn't feel any jet lag. And I ate with gusto too. Well, Belmonte, it seems you're still a Chilean, I said to myself, digging into my roast beef.

"Galo," "Moreira," or whatever his name was must have rented a P.O. box in some neighborhood post office, but not his own. And not near where he worked. His hiding the key in the hollow beam suggested the P.O. box was important. It would have to be a post office with a lot of traffic, but not the main one. Before paying, I asked for a phone book and looked at the long list of Santiago post offices.

I chose the post office on Avenida Matta because it was in the heart of a business district. Nothing doing there, or at the post office by the central market. Clever guy, Galo. It took me three hours to find the right P.O. It shared a building with city offices, a bank, and a shopping center.

I opened the box. It was empty. After checking out the staff, I decided to try bluffing. I went up to the oldest worker.

"Sir, pardon me, what's the new woman's name?"

"Which one? There are two new women. The blonde?"

"No, the other one."

"Ah, Jacqueline. Her name is Jacqueline."

"Thanks. I couldn't remember. Thanks."

"Of course, she's so new . . ."

Thank goodness for the custom that requires postal employees to wear a plastic badge with their names.

I went up to the window where J. Gatica was on duty, and continued bluffing.

"Miss, can you help me?"

"What is it, sir?"

"I have a P.O. box and I'm expecting a letter from Germany. It's from my brother, you see, and it contains important papers. The funny thing is I phoned him yesterday and he told me he sent the letter two weeks ago. What can have happened?"

"What's your name?"

"Bonifacio Prado Cifuentes, Box 2722."

J. Gatica went to look in a thick notebook. She made a note on a slip of paper and returned to her station.

"You already got that letter, Señor Prado. We put it in your box nine days ago. It was from Berlin, Alexanderplatz, and the sender's initials were W.S."

"How odd. Maybe my wife picked it up and forgot to give it to me."

"That must be what happened, Señor Prado."

Santiago was a new city for me in many regards. Some changes I was glad to see, such as the proliferation of telephones in the subway stations. Five in the afternoon in Chile. Ten at night in Hamburg. Kramer expected my call from Tierra del Fuego at midnight. I got in early.

"Belmonte. How is everything? Where are you?"

"Everything's off. I'm in Santiago."

"What the hell is going on?"

"Listen, Kramer. I want you to use your contacts with the top cops. I want you to find out if they have anything on a guy with the initials W.S. I think he's the Major's man."

"All right. Find a hotel and call me right back."

The top cops' computers function with great efficiency in Germany. I took Kramer's call at eight that night in my room at the Hotel Santa Lucía. The cripple was beside himself with joy.

"Belmonte? Bingo."

"Out with it, quick."

"W.S. Werner Schroeders. That was the cover of a GDR intelligence officer based at Cottbus. His real name is Frank Galinsky, and that's not all. He flew to Santiago four days ago. Tomorrow you leave for Tierra del Fuego. There's not a moment to lose."

"There's one problem, Kramer."

"What's that?"

"The guy has a gun, a nine-millimeter."

"Impossible. No one can get weapons onto a Luf-thansa plane."

"He bought it here. And murdered the seller."

"We have a deal, Belmonte. Tomorrow you call me from down south."

"I'll keep my end of the deal, Kramer. But I'm going to do it in my own way."

I watched night fall over Santiago. And Verónica was near, so near, my love, and me dreading our reunion, but that dread was slowly giving way. And what kept me from rushing into your arms, Verónica my love, was just this crazy need to finish what I start, and the coming challenge, that set me on a path I thought I'd forgotten, the path that would take me back to what I used to be, the man you loved.

Part Three

*. . . since only fools could care about something unrelated
to the art of staying alive.*

MARCIO SOUZA,
ending of *Mad Maria*

CHAPTER ONE

Tierra del Fuego: A Final Farewell

Griselda was in a chair next to the fireplace, and to the right of the dead man. Dr. Aguirre and her son, Jacinto, sat beside her. Sitting in a row on the other side of the coffin were: Mansur, who ran the boardinghouse, and his wife, Ana, the deaf-mute; Santos Ledesma the gelder, Sergeants Gálvez and Bryce, of the carabineros, who had come on the unusual assignment of preserving public order.

Each member of the company had offered sincere condolences, to which Griselda listened shamefaced at first, because they confirmed unfounded rumors that made her old Franz's concubine. Rumors she soon admitted, however, were true. After all, life owed her a proper wake, with a dead man of her own presiding over the ceremonies with his waxen face. She had not been able to see her late husband's face before they buried him. He was in his diver's suit, and sealed off from the world in half a ton of ice.

"I don't understand why he did it. I saw him a few days ago, when he was redoing the roof. I offered to help him and he replied that there are things a man must do alone. He looked fine. I don't understand it, but I respect it," said Santos Ledesma.

"Was he sad lately?" asked Mansur.

"No. I was with him before . . . well. He wanted to eat roast goat and I fixed it for him. He drank his wine and listened to the music he likes. He was even joking before I left him," Griselda sobbed.

"It's not Christian behavior, to blow your brains out, forgive me, Señora," Bryce of the national police gave as his opinion.

"But it takes a real man to do something like that," Sergeant Gálvez disagreed.

"Shall we change the subject?" Dr. Aguirre suggested.

"You're right, Doctor. Come, my little mute."

Mansur and his wife moved over to the fireplace. Griselda was about to get up too, but Mansur motioned gently for her to remain seated.

The mute woman heaped the embers and set a kettle of oil to heating, and when it reached the boiling point, she dropped in the turnovers she had prepared and brought with her. She fried them one by one, those empanadas with onion but no meat that are an indispensable part of every wake on Tierra del Fuego.

They ate leaning forward, to keep the thick gravy from staining their clothes. Mansur poured the wine and the tray of glasses passed from hand to hand.

"You sure know how to make turnovers, Mansur," said Sergeant Gálvez.

"I make the filling. The real art is in the crust, and that's my wife's job," Mansur answered, patting his companion's arm.

"You have the hands of a nun, Señora," Bryce the policeman complimented her.

The deaf-mute looked at Mansur with a question in her eyes.

"He says you have the hands of a nun."

She smiled and hastened back to the fireplace to fry more turnovers.

"To the deceased. May he rest in peace," Griselda proposed.

The others agreed, raising their glasses in silence.

Jacinto and Dr. Aguirre stepped outside for some fresh air. The sky was intensely blue. They raised their heads to watch a flock of bustards flying north. They trekked to a hilltop with a view of Useless Bay in all its immensity.

"The sea is changing color. Another winter," the doctor remarked.

"Listen, what's this about the will? I still don't understand it."

"It's very simple. The old man left everything he had to your mother. The house, the lot, the livestock. But the will has one rather special clause. Your mother may not sell the house or make any changes."

"For how long?"

"Forever. But if one day Griselda leaves us, then everything is yours and you can do what you want."

"What a crock. I never liked the old man, Doctor. I always considered him an impostor, someone who was trying to take my father's place. And I moved to Punta Arenas because I couldn't stand the gossip going around, about my mother and him. This inheritance makes my mother the old man's official widow. If he loved her so much, why didn't he marry her?"

"You're very foolish, Jacinto. Your mother and the old man had something very beautiful and deep between them. It's called friendship. Friendship between two beings with a lot of living behind them. It's usually more interesting than love."

On returning to the house, they saw a third horse tied up next to the policemen's mounts. It was the priest's old nag. It looked like a hairy dwarf alongside the policemen's spirited steeds.

The priest sampled a couple of turnovers, praising them mightily. He downed a quick glass of wine, draped his stole around his neck, and approached the coffin.

"In the name of the Father, the Son, and the Holy Ghost. I absolve you of all your sins, brother Franz. We know little enough about you, there may be many facts about your life we'll never learn, but perhaps it's God's will that this immense land should be full of secrets. You committed the worst of all sins; with your own hands you ended your life, which only the Lord can take from you. Nevertheless I absolve you. God never looks to Tierra del Fuego. Amen."

CHAPTER TWO

Tierra del Fuego: The Dropout

When we landed in Punta Arenas, I was grateful for the anorak Pedro de Valdivia had provided. The sun shone brightly, but was robbed of its heat by gusts of icy, briny wind whipping at trees and bodies.

I had no trouble reaching the dock or finding my way to the doors of Five Men on a Dead Man's Chest. I had never been in this southern city before, but in Hamburg I'd heard dozens of sailors mention Five Men on a Dead Man's Chest as a great hangout for seafaring folk.

The moment I crossed the threshhold, I felt the welcoming warmth from the salamander stove burning in the center of the room. From the kitchen came the appetizing aroma of lamb stew. The long bar was of shiny, well-polished wood. Hundreds of bottles were lined up behind it, along with astrolabes, compasses, pennants, and other tools of the mariner's trade.

"The lamb will be a while yet," the waiter greeted me.

"I can wait."

"Thirsty?"

"Give me something to warm my bones."

"Cane liquor's what you want."

There were a good dozen men sitting at several tables. They were talking about the price of shellfish, and cursing the Japanese fishing fleet. I took my glass of brandy to an empty table. A stout guy turned around to talk to me.

"Do you play truco, countryman? We need a fourth hand."

"Someone who's ready to buy us lunch," added another man, wearing an oilman's silvery helmet.

"No, I'm sorry. I always wanted to learn but I never had a chance."

"All right, if you want to learn by losing, draw up a chair," the husky fellow invited me.

I joined their table. The third man was smoking a pipe. He began to shuffle the cards.

It was true. I had always wanted to learn how to play truco, but it was also true that now the opportunity arose, I wasn't in the mood for card games. Such is life.

"I have a friend who's a truco player. He's one of the best," I said.

"From Patagonia or Fuego?" the husky guy asked.

"From here, from Punta Arenas," I replied.

"From Patagonia, then. And what's your friend's name, if one might ask?" the pipe smoker inquired.

"Cano, Carlos Cano. Do you know him?"

"Cano, the one from the *Pearl of the South,*" the husky fellow said.

"The same. Do you know if he's in town?"

"And do you know if he wants us telling you?" inquired the man in the shiny helmet.

"I'll bet you lunch that he'll be glad to see me."

"You're on. If he's not glad to see you, we'll buy you a new set of teeth, because you're going to need it," the husky fellow said, accepting my offer.

The guy with the shiny helmet left, saying he'd be back in half an hour. The other two invited me to switch from brandy to the wine they were drinking.

"Now we're down to three again. Shall we play dominoes?" The pipe smoker proposed.

We played a few rounds of dominoes. I could sense the guys watching me out of the corner of one eye. I tried to play as best I could, while wondering how Cano would react when he saw me.

Carlos Cano. I've rarely met anyone with his sense of humor. He could crack jokes in the midst of the most appalling situations. Cano was the only man from Fuego in the FOA, the group of Salvador Allende's personal friends, the late president's private guard. They called him the Yagan, or the Kanasaka Iceberg, and he was always a man of courage as cool as the part of the world he came from. As a member of the FOA he took part in the battle at the

Moneda Palace that September 11, 1973. Nearly the whole group died fighting alongside Allende. Cano managed to save his own life by playing dead. With two bullets in his body, he lay among his fallen comrades and held his breath while army officers went around killing off the wounded. But he survived that hell, and as soon as he was out of downtown Santiago he jumped clear of the truck loaded with corpses. Limping and weakened by loss of blood, he reached the San Joaquin industrial belt, where people were still battling a brutal soldiery on the rampage.

There a doctor examined him, shaking his head in disbelief.

"You've got one bullet in your gut and another in your shoulder," he told him.

"That figures. I got off a few myself," he replied.

Cano managed to get away to Argentina in November 1973. The failure of the Montoneros in Argentina and Fuerzas Armadas Revolucionarias in Colombia added to his growing disenchantment with politics. And finally, he suffered through the mop-up of the Simón Bolívar International Brigade in Nicaragua.

I'd seen him last in Malmö, in 1985. He was working the tiller on a little ferry that linked this Swedish port with Copenhagen.

"One more year and I'm taking off. I've saved enough money to buy a boat. A fantastic boat," he told me over a few beers.

"In Chile?"

"Yes, but way down south. I'll never venture farther north than the Strait of Magellan."

"And what about the cause?"

"It can go to hell. Without me. I'm dropping out."

Five years later I saw him again, on German television. A German ship was searching for sunken treasure in waters just north of the Antarctic Ocean. Cano was at the tiller.

The man in the shiny helmet entered the bar first and pointed a finger at me. Cano came in behind him. He saw me and covered his eyes. Right away, he motioned me over to the bar.

"No. Whatever it is, my answer is no," he said.

"Be glad to see me or I'll have to buy lunch for those three guys."

"And a brandy for me. What are you mixed up in, Belmonte?"

"Nothing illegal. It's just a job, plain and simple."

"How did you find me?"

"I didn't forget what you told me in Malmö, then I saw you on German television, and half an hour ago I dropped your name to your pals. Very easy."

"And you wanted to see me because I'm cute. Come on, spit it out."

"It's a long story. Shall we sit down?"

"All right. But don't forget you're talking to a drop-out."

While the three would-be card players devoured the lamb stew I insisted on treating them to, Cano and I sat at a table some distance away. There we did what all veterans are wont to do who have been accomplices in losing battles. We didn't talk about the battles, but about how surprised we were to be alive at all.

I told him what had brought me to this far corner of the earth, the deal with Kramer, the story of the gold coins, Galo's death, entailing the possibility of a second person interested in the booty, and finally I told him about Verónica.

"It's not the only case. I'm sorry, Belmonte. I'm truly sorry."

"I believe you. I need you to give me a hand."

"If I can, I'll do it, although I can't help liking the German. I too dreamed of finding Galo and making him pay for what happened in Nicaragua."

"You know this area. You can save me time."

"I know it somewhat. Tierra del Fuego is a very big place, Belmonte. And besides, it's full of secrets. Your story proves it."

"Our friend Franz Stahl, who must be in his seventies by now, receives his mail at Post Box Number Five. Does that say anything to you?"

"Not much. That's somewhere between Puerto Nuevo and Tres Vistas."

"Greek to me. Explain yourself."

"Puerto Nuevo is a little fishing cove. They used to be whalers, but since the whales disappeared—the Japanese wiped them out—the people down there concentrate on small-scale fishing, and a shellfish operation. There must be about twenty families. Tres Vistas is about fifty kilometers from Puerto Nuevo. It's a truck stop with all of two houses. One functions as a general store and the other as a boardinghouse. I know the owner of the boardinghouse. He's a guy from up north, name of Mansur. From what you tell me I figure that the German must live closer to Tres Vistas than to Puerto Nuevo, because the cove has its own post office. I have an idea, Belmonte. Pour me another glass of wine. I'm beginning to see the light."

We left Five Men on a Dead Man's Chest and headed to the Magellan district office. On the way, Cano spoke proudly of the *Pearl of the South*, a three-masted boat he had purchased with his savings from Scandinavia. He lived on and from the boat. In winter he docked at the sportsmen's marina in Punta Arenas and in summer he took tourists on excursions along Cape Horn.

"And I hunt for treasure. I found a good collection of Spanish cannons and all kinds of junk the museums pay good money for. One of these days I'll run into the treasure of Sir Francis Drake."

"It all sounds good, but it smacks of misogyny."

"Don't believe it. I spend the summers in good company. My wife is a diver. She spends the winters up north,

in Arica, as a warm-water scuba diving instructor for tourists. It's better that way. There's nothing like spending the
winter with a keg of brandy and the complete works of
Simenon. If you'd arrived two days ago you would have
met her. Her name is Nilda and she leaves World's End
along with the first bustards. Look. There's a whole flock
of them on the wing. Winter is coming, big guy."

In the district office Cano asked to speak with someone who was clearly a big shot. There was no other way
to explain the courteous reception we got from a national
police official. We waited around five minutes and then
the official opened an imposingly armored door. The man
behind the mahogany desk stood up the moment he saw
Carlos.

"Carlitos, what a pleasant surprise," he said.

"This is my friend Juan Belmonte. Belmonte, Señor
Marchenko, in charge of oil drilling in the Magellan district."

"Juan Belmonte. Did you know that's the name of a
bullfighter?" he said, holding out his right hand.

"Really? That's the first I've ever heard of it."

After introducing us, Carlos indicated that I was an
insurance agent interested in settling a matter of inheritance. He added that I had come from Germany, looking
for someone named Franz Stahl, and that unfortunately I
had only his mailing address. Marchenko said that locating
a home address in Tierra del Fuego was easy, as long as

the person sought was a landowner. He left us for a few minutes and returned with a map, which he spread out on the desk.

"This is the southeast coast of Tierra del Fuego. Franz Stahl owns a plot of land situated fifteen kilometers from Tres Vistas. To get there you need an all-terrain vehicle or a horse. Can I do anything else for you, Señor Belmonte?"

"No, you've already done more than enough. Thank you."

"Juan Belmonte. It must be comforting to have the same name as a famous bullfighter. There aren't many Belmontes in Chile, and there are even fewer of us Marchenkos," he said as we took our leave.

"That may be lucky for the country, in the case of the Belmontes."

We left the district office with the information I needed. Cano was smiling. We set out toward the harbor.

"Not bad, that remark about the Belmontes."

"I meant it. What sort of fellow is he?"

"Marchenko isn't a bad guy. He's a ceremonious idiot and he sends me tourists in summer."

"Is he related to the other Marchenko?"

"His brother. He knows I was a member of the FOA; everyone knows everything here. He's scared shitless, so he tries to be friendly. His brother is still in the army. He's a colonel now. A number of torture victims have recognized him, but he's one of the untouchables."

"The price of democracy. It's hard to believe I'm in Chile. I never intended to return. I held back because I was scared of bumping into guys like him, the ones who always knew what was happening, didn't lift a finger to stop it, and concentrated on getting rich on the quiet while others did the dirty work for them. I suppose now he's one of those champions of democracy, capable of admitting that things got out of hand a little. Sickening, the price of democracy."

"That's how it is. But it's a relative price. Not a month goes by that some official involved in torture and disappearances isn't pumped full of lead in broad daylight. There's still a wholesome element in this country."

"I don't give a crap about this country, Cano. You haven't told me where we're going."

"To the boat. I'm going to leave you on the other side of the Strait. Consider yourself a guest aboard the *Pearl of the South.*"

We crossed the Strait, Cano's boat gliding through a calm sea. The edge of its keel plowed a delicate furrow of foam. Besides Cano there were two other crew members on board. From the bridge, I watched them handle the sails with assurance. They were men of few words. I suddenly envied Carlos Cano's life. I could sense how he trusted these men, and I could smell their trust in his skill at the wheel. Together, they got where they wanted to go. They set goals and they reached them. Few people can afford that luxury in life.

The crossing lasted nearly three hours. Toward evening, we anchored at the Puerto Nuevo pier, in Useless Bay. Cano ordered his men to put ashore a motorcycle.

"All right, here you are, Belmonte. The motorcycle has a full tank. You already know what you have to do. You can make it from here to Tres Vistas in an hour. There, you'll say hello to Mansur for me. He'll show you how to get to the German's house."

"Thanks, Cano. When this is over I'll take the ferry back to Punta Arenas, and return the motorcycle. See you soon."

"Good luck."

I revved up the motorcycle, an all-terrain job with a powerful roar. I was adjusting the helmet when I heard Cano calling to me from the boat.

"Belmonte, take a look in the toolbox. Under the seat."

I lifted the seat. Among an assortment of wrenches, I found a .765 Browning. I waved back at Cano.

"It's not healthy to go through life naked," he shouted from the deck.

A few minutes later I left Puerto Nuevo behind. The road ran through the pampas, straight as an arrow, and I was headed for the arrow's tip.

CHAPTER THREE

Tierra del Fuego: Sunset

Galinsky had come a long way to reach the top of the hill. Now he was taking a rest, lying facedown in the grass, keeping an eye on the house in the hollow.

From Berlin to Frankfurt, from there to Santiago, and then on to Punta Arenas, and finally across the Strait. Now here he was, five hundred yards from his goal. He opened his knapsack, took out a chocolate bar, and started chewing slowly. Then he took a few sips from a bottle of mineral water and lit a cigarette. While he was smoking, his thoughts turned to the unexpected difficulties he'd been having. A series of unforeseen events, the inevitable imponderables, were beginning to interfere with the plan. And since the only way to head off this interference was by analyzing it, he decided to take stock of the situation.

Poor Moreira. His original idea had been to recruit

him and put him to work, while he, Galinsky, remained in the background, making the decisions. A Chilean had a better chance of going unnoticed. But he found him a changed man, a hysteric, the kind of person who couldn't be trusted. When he plugged him between the eyes, he had some idea of the trouble in store for him, operating on his own, especially because, in order to ascertain Hans Hillermann's false identity, he would be obliged to interrogate several people. He didn't know whom, but it was no secret that Tierra del Fuego had a large German colony, and sometimes a compatriot can turn talkative. In any case, his fears were dispelled when he phoned the Major from Punta Arenas.

"First step, OK. But no one knows anything about Hillermann. There's no one receiving mail under that name," Galinsky said.

"That figures. Our collector's name is Franz Stahl. A rather original name. Glad to hear it?"

"Thrilled. Thanks for the tip."

The Major was still a model of efficiency. Galinsky, lying stretched out in the grass, told himself there was no point in wondering how the Major had obtained that information, but then he considered how he would have done it himself.

Let's review the facts. Ulrich Helm, cripple though he was, outsmarted us coming and going. You might even say that, without our realizing it, he directed his own interrogation. Skillfully deflecting our questions, he kept us from reaching the most important one: Hillermann's new identity. But he knew all along that we were bound to ask about that; it was only a matter of time. So then what did he do? He got away from us twice. The first time he faked a heart attack right in the street, and the second time, in the hospital, he slit his wrists. Someone that loyal doesn't abandon a friend in danger, without alerting him . . . That's it: he wrote to him. Somehow he got the letter out of the hospital. After that, it was just a matter of chatting with the doctors or the nurses.

Galinsky rubbed his arms. He felt a need to get up and move around a little, to get his blood circulating, to replace the warmth he was losing. He yawned, and promptly slapped his face hard. Perhaps, he thought, it hadn't been a good idea to make the trip from Porvenir to Tres Vistas at night.

In Porvenir, the agency where he rented the Land Rover told him it would be easy to get to Tres Vistas, where they would tell him how to reach his friend Franz Stahl's spread.

"It's a five- or six-hour trip. With a spare can of gasoline you'll have enough for the round-trip," the agent told him.

Galinsky set out shortly after midnight. A full moon lit the lonely road, so that he barely needed the headlights. He was nervous and cheerful at the same time. He sensed that his body was about to enter the serene state indispensable to a successful mission.

The road was rough and full of potholes and the moon shone brightly on a vast landscape, monotonous and desolate; one long unbroken stretch of gray splotches and a few barberry bushes. But Galinsky hadn't traveled twelve thousand miles to enjoy the scenery in Tierra del Fuego. He was ready for action; the familiar obsessive impulse primed his muscles and gave him, as he hastily confirmed, patting his crotch, a tormenting erection. He remembered having read somewhere about erections, or even involuntary ejaculations, occurring unexpectedly in hunters at the critical moment in the hunt, when their attention is entirely focused on their prey, and the rhythm of their breathing accelerates as they close in for the kill. "And not only hunters," he murmured. Soldiers too. Alexander the Great ordered his officers to observe the warriors' crotches before entering the fray.

He made slow headway in the Land Rover, avoiding large potholes and suspiciously deep puddles. And so the first light of dawn overtook him. The moon went on shining, as if it doubted the regular habit of the sun just beginning to emerge from the waters of the Atlantic. Galinsky kept his eyes on the rough road. He had turned off the headlights. Concentrated on his driving, he didn't see the lapwings, numb with cold, casting hateful glances from the tops of telegraph poles, or the abundant flocks of herons that began to plow the sky in a northeasterly direction once the sun had risen in full splendor. Those birds came from far off, as far or even farther than Galinsky, from the Falklands or the South Georgia Islands, to shelter in the fjords at the north end of the Brunswick peninsula.

At a little after six in the morning, he stopped the car. He was in Tres Vistas. The place was just as they had described it at the car-rental agency: two houses on opposite sides of a road, trying to look like a street.

He knocked at the door of the boardinghouse first, obtaining no response. Then he tried the general store and was waited on by an old man who gave him a look that was half friendly, half suspicious.

"All I can offer you are maté and biscuits," the old man began.

"I'm not hungry. I'm looking for a friend who lives near here."

"The thing is, they're all out. I don't know where they went. Could be they told me, but I forgot. I forget everything. Aguirre says it's old age. Would you like me to kill a chicken?"

"My friend's name is Franz Stahl, do you understand? He's a German."

"I may know him. Can't say. Just now I don't recall. If you don't like fowl we can slaughter a lamb, but you'll have to help me. I don't have the strength."

"Can I talk to someone else?"

"No. I already told you, they're all out."

"Who are they all?"

"My son-in-law Mansur, my daughter the mute, Dr. Aguirre, and the gelder."

"Where did they go?"

"Who?"

"Mansur, the gelder, your daughter."

"I don't remember. They went off, and they told me: we're going, none of your little tricks. I knew where they were headed, but I forgot. Shall we kill a lamb?"

Galinsky stretched out an arm, grabbed the old man by the scruff of his neck, and shook him violently, till he could hear his moaning mingled with the painful rattling of his bones. He saw panic in the old man's eyes.

"Listen, you old bag of shit. Franz Stahl, the German. How do I get to his house? Franz Stahl. Franz Stahl. Repeat it with me."

"Franz . . . unhand me, ruffian. Now I remember."

"Start talking. How do I get to Franz Stahl's house?"

"You follow the road to the mail drop. Then you cut through the pampas till you come to the ravine. At the end of it, you can see the house. Where's your horse?"

"Listen, you imbecile, to get to the German's house I follow the road all the way to the mail drop, and then head into the pampas till I come to the ravine, is that it?"

"If you know, why the hell do you ask? What do we do about the lamb?"

Galinsky let go of the old man. He left him muttering curses because no one would help him slaughter a lamb. He went to the Land Rover, took out a map of the area, and opened it on the seat of the car. It was possible the old man had given him correct information. He saw the dot indicating the mail drop at the side of the road. To the south was a short stretch of pampas, and then the sea. To the north, he saw the symbol for uneven terrain, either a gully or a ravine. Much farther north ran winding China Creek, a river rising in the slopes of the Boquerón range. A number of tiny squares were the symbol for cattle ranches scattered along the river. A tiny circle at the end of the ravine must be the house he was looking for. The old man tapped him on the arm.

"Now I remember," he said.

"How to get to the German?"

"They went to the wake. Everyone went to the wake."

"Whose wake?"

"Your friend the German. My sincerest condolences."

The old man, hand outstretched, was left standing in the middle of the road. He coughed and rubbed his eyes, the better to see the car move off in a cloud of dust.

At the top of the hill, Galinsky began to do some relaxation exercises. First he bent his toes, then he filled his lungs with air and let it out slowly while flexing his toes. Then he repeated the exercise, tensing his calf muscles, his thighs, his backside, his stomach, all the way up to his eyebrows. When he was through he felt a wave of well-being wash over him. It allowed him to forget, temporarily, the seven hours he had spent lying in the grass.

He had left Tres Vistas at six-thirty in the morning. On the dot of eight he spotted the mail drop, perched on pilings, and cut into the pampas. It was rough going until he reached the ravine. The wheels slid on the slick grass and he almost lost control of the car several times. He abandoned the Land Rover where the ravine began. It was impossible to drive any farther on that slippery grass, so he threw the knapsack over his shoulder and walked on at a rapid pace, until nine-thirty in the morning. The ravine led to the hill where he had been keeping watch over the house in the hollow. He was separated from it by some three hundred yards of pampas.

It looked as if the old man in Tres Vistas had become coherent just in the nick of time. Galinsky, on the hilltop, observed the house through a pair of binoculars. He counted nine horses tied up outside. Two stood out as larger and more graceful than the rest. They were elegant horses. The others were smaller and shaggier. Inspecting the saddles lined up on the porch, he discovered that two of them displayed the insignia of the Chilean national police, a pair of crossed rifles. Later he saw two men in uniform come out of the house, in the company of a gray-haired individual, and take a short walk. Eight people in all had come out of the house and gone back in again, after spending time in a hut at some distance from the house, at the end of a plank path lined with apple trees. Two of those present were women. Galinsky laid out eight matches on the grass and assigned them the characteristics he noted in the inhabitants, as they appeared and then disappeared again beneath the tin roof.

The sun had begun its downward course over the Pacific. Galinsky had another go at his chocolate bar.

Life is strange, he said to himself. I came here, all set to eliminate a man, only to find that he's already dead. What can have happened to him? Some ailment of old age? An accident? Did he receive a warning from his loyal friend Ulrich Helm, and it gave him heart failure?

From the moment he laid eyes on it, Galinsky had no doubt as to the owner of the house. He studied the wooden building through his binoculars, pausing at the window frames. He saw they all had the same carving, the door with triple towers crowned by two stars of David and a Christian cross. Homesickness or force of habit gave Hans Hillermann away. It could have been a house in Bergedorf, Curslack, or any dinky hamlet on the Elbe. Only the shiny tin roof broke faith with a familiar architecture.

Frank Galinsky saw the sun shining like a great ball of fire in the west. He calculated that he had about two hours of daylight left. Still wondering what the hell they were doing with the dead man, he took a thin sleeping bag from his knapsack. He slipped inside it, until only his head was left uncovered, and brought the binoculars to his eyes. He looked like a giant worm gazing at the sunset, but in fact Galinsky was staring at the two men who had just left the house. They moved about a hundred yards off, and began to dig a rectangular pit.

CHAPTER FOUR

Tierra del Fuego: The Long Southern Night

The two buildings that comprised Tres Vistas looked like the eye of a needle looming in the middle of the road. I arrived at the hour when shadows take possession of the landscape. The two houses were of wood, and their thatched roofs gave them the look of slumbering beasts. One house was adorned with an unusual advertisement for Monkey brand anisette. Right below the buttocks of Charles Darwin's monkey twin was a shop sign announcing, in black lettering, GENERAL STORE: A LITTLE OF EVERYTHING. The other house displayed a discreet notice, painted on a small board, PENSIÓN MANSUR. There was no light to be seen in either house. Before turning off the motor I sounded the horn. An old man popped out of the general store, carrying a carbide lamp.

"They're not here. There's no one home," he said, squinting at me.

"You're someone, grandpa."

"Come in. If you want something, take it and write down the price. They told me none of my tricks and not to try running the business."

I followed him, doubtful. It didn't look as if this old man would be easy to talk to. He opened the door of the shop and offered me a seat. Inside it smelled of spices, coffee, maté tea, tobacco, and the thousand items neatly arranged in crates and display cases, amidst farm implements, jugs, buckets, and riding gear. He handed me a big gourd of maté.

"Are you hungry? If you want, I can kill a chicken, one of my own. Or would you like a piece of lamb?"

"The maté is enough. Thank you. Grandpa, I'm looking for a German . . ."

"We're all searching for something in this life. I searched too, but I don't know what for . . . I forgot. Everything slips my mind. Aguirre says I shouldn't eat meat."

"Who is Aguirre?"

"Aguirre? The doctor. He treats our sheep for mange and our cows for hoof-and-mouth disease. Sometimes he treats people too. Why are you looking for the German?"

"Do you know him? I have a message for him. It's urgent."

"Who knows. I might know him. I don't recall just now. Wait for my son-in-law. He knows everyone."

"Where is your son-in-law? Can I call him?"

"He went away. They all went away. But they'll be back. Be patient."

"Do you know where they went?"

"They told me, but I forgot. I already told you, I forget everything. There are hard-boiled eggs. Shall I bring you a couple?"

The old man went into the next room. In a little while he came back with a tray of hard-boiled eggs and a marmoreal-looking slab of bread; the hardtack of gauchos. He summoned me to a table. On the counter were several bottles of Argentine wine. I took one and went over to the old man.

"Eat. I didn't hear your horse. Where did you leave it?"

"I'm on a motorcycle. Do you know what a motorcycle is?"

"Poppycock. Sissy stuff. Real men ride horses."

"Grandpa, help me. The German I'm looking for is named Franz Stahl and he lives around here. Do you know him?"

"I don't recall. I have known many Germans, good men and scoundrels. Such is life. If everyone were good, it would be very boring. I have also known gringos and Croats. North of the Strait it's full of Croats. I don't like them."

"Have a glass of wine, grandpa. Franz Stahl. Franz, maybe they call him Francisco."

"Francisco was a chief. Francisco Calfucurá. That I

remember. From when you saw Indians around here. Now there are none left. The gringos killed them. Scoundrels. The Croats killed Indians too. Like I said, I don't like them. They eat rabbits. Jerks. Why harm those poor little creatures, when we have so much lamb? Do you play truco? When my son-in-law and the doctor come back, we could play a few hands."

That old man's memories were as scattered as the pieces in a kaleidoscope, and setting them in order looked like a time-consuming job. Listening to him come out with sentences that made a lot of sense to him, I thought of you, Verónica, my love. Did the same thing happen to you? Was your distracted silence a world of crystals that no one, not even you yourself, could arrange in their exact geometric form? But at least that old man was talking, while you, my love, had lost even the architecture of speech.

As I was drinking that strong, sour wine, I heard dogs barking and the sound of horses' hooves approaching. The old man lit some lamps.

A heavyset man was the first to enter, followed by a small bright-eyed woman, and then another individual with gray hair and tortoiseshell glasses with thick lenses. They seemed surprised to see me.

"He owes for some eggs and a bottle of wine," said the old man.

"That's fine, father-in-law. Go to bed," said the heavyset man.

"Are you Mansur, who runs the boardinghouse?"

"Yes, the boardinghouse and the general store are both mine. Were you looking for me?"

"Carlos Cano sent me. He said you could help me."

"What about you, do you have a name too?"

"Belmonte, Juan Belmonte."

"Like the bullfighter. I'm Romualdo Aguirre. Sawbones," the man in the tortoiseshell glasses introduced himself.

"Ana, my wife. She's mute, but she hears well. As long as you raise your voice a little," said Mansur, offering me his hand.

"I'm looking for a German. His name is Franz Stahl. Do you know him?"

The folks who had just come in looked at one another. Mansur touched his wife's arm and she went into the next room.

"You've come too late, countryman. Doctor, you talk to our friend. I'm going to unsaddle the horses."

Romualdo Aguirre picked up three glasses and sat down at a table. He offered me a cigarette. He poured the wine and shook his head, before speaking.

"I suppose you've come from Germany."

"Let's speak plainly, Doctor. How do you know?"

"I don't know. I'm just guessing. The man you're looking for, Franz Stahl, is dead. We buried him a few hours ago. He blew his brains out with a shotgun."

Galinsky's name was on the tip of my tongue. I had

arrived too late. It's very easy to fake a suicide with a shotgun.

"When did it happen?"

"Last night. He was acting very strangely the last few days. Were you the one asking for someone named Hallmann or Hillman, in the Punta Arenas post office?"

"No, but I think I know who you're talking about. So he was acting strangely. What else?"

"That's not the way. You're the one who should be answering questions," Mansur said from the doorway.

Ana joined the group too. With energetic hands she cut chunks of sheep's milk cheese, bread, and pieces of *charqui,* that gamy dried horsemeat my taste buds had forgotten. Mansur uncorked another bottle of wine. I felt exposed to the verdict of a jury, and while I sought the right words to describe the man they had just laid in the ground, the inexplicable something that haunts the deaths of those who have lived intensely told me that in the German's death there was much to suggest a hand well played, a trump card, a sarcastic grimace directed at Kramer, the Major, Galinsky, Galo, and all the other bastards in such a hurry to hunt him down. And that same indescribable something made me see in his death a friend's, a comrade's wink, dedicated to Ulrich Helm, the other hero of this tale, who'd had a harder time of it. And so I began by revealing Franz Stahl's true identity to them, and then, faithful to the times that formed me and to which I owe the bitterness I camouflage as toughness, I told them the story of those two antifascists who dreamed of utopian freedom in Tierra del Fuego and who, to attain it, did not hesitate to steal the eggs out of the eagle's very nest.

In total silence, except for the snoring of the old man, who had refused to leave the table, they listened to the story of a friendship, a loyalty that had withstood every test unharmed, including the most dreaded: the test of time.

"We never saw a gram of gold on him. Everything he owned was the work of his own hands." Aguirre sighed.

"Sixty-three gold coins?" Mansur couldn't believe it.

"Each weighing ten ounces. Their value is beyond reckoning. They must be somewhere," I added.

"I'm not interested. We live quietly here, with what we have. What do you say, Doctor?" Mansur asked.

"I like legends. These coins will be one more legend. Tierra del Fuego is full of hidden treasures. There's room for one more."

Ana struck the table and, fixing Mansur with a stare, began to gesticulate. Her eyes shone, her gestures were emphatic, admitting of no argument. Mansur nodded in agreement.

"I think my wife is right. This gold will bring misfortune. Franz's death was the first. We've got to find it before we have an epidemic. She wants to know who was the man asking for Franz in Punta Arenas."

I told them what I knew of Galinsky, from the trail he left behind him in Santiago.

"Two deaths," Aguirre remarked.

"Three. Don't forget Ulrich Helm. I think as she does. These coins will only bring trouble. All right. I've told you everything I know, now I want to know the details. How did Hillermann, or whatever you prefer to call him, die?"

"From the time he heard that someone had asked for him, well, we only just found that out, he turned strange," Aguirre began. "We were friends; he was held in high regard by everyone around here. About four days ago he startled me by asking for my help in drawing up a will. He left all his possessions to Griselda, a widow woman who kept him company for twenty years or so. I wrote down what he dictated, I signed as a witness, and I turned it over to the notary in Porvenir. That was the last time I saw him. Griselda is the one who knows, she was with him yesterday evening. As always, she went to fix him something to eat, and she left him at around ten at night. She says she left him in good shape, perhaps a bit cheery from all the wine he'd drunk with his meal. She left him. She had gone about half a mile when, suddenly, one of those intuitions women get made her turn back. She was just outside the house when she heard the explosion. She found him dead, with the rifle still between his legs. I examined the body and I can assure you he committed suicide. Griselda left the house and rode right here to let us know of the terrible doings. What else happened? We left almost at once and reached Franz's house before dawn. Ledesma was with us last night, a sheep gelder who makes the rounds of the ranches. We sent him to Puerto Nuevo to notify the police. Later he joined us again, with a couple of policemen," Aguirre ended his tale.

"I must go to the house of the deceased. Can you help me?"

"Of course. Wait for daybreak and we'll leave. The horses need a few hours of rest," said Mansur, but was unable to continue because at that very moment we heard the hoofbeats of a horse approaching at a gallop.

Mansur went out the door.

"Doctor. It's Griselda's horse," he called from outside.

Ana covered her mouth with her hands.

"Damn. We left Griselda all alone out there," Aguirre muttered.

We leapt from our chairs. The noise woke the grandfather.

"Old Franz. You want to go to Old Franz's place too. Don't hit me. I'll tell you how to get there," he moaned, appealing to Ana for protection.

"Calm down, grandpa. You're dreaming," Aguirre said.

"No, the other man who asked for old Franz hit me. Now I remember. Don't let them hit me."

"When did the other man hit you, grandpa? Try to remember. When?"

"I don't know. He came in a green car. He didn't have a horse."

We went outside. Mansur cursed the exhausted state of his horses. Aguirre took a lamp and we rushed to check the road. We had no trouble finding tire tracks. And Galinsky had left one huge clue. At the side of the road lay a shiny pack of that most German brand of cigarettes: Revals.

"Where to?" I asked, already mounted on the motorcycle.

"Straight ahead to the mail drop. Then follow the ravine. We'll follow you in an hour," Aguirre replied.

It was just beginning to grow light when I hit the structure raised on pilings. Before leaving the road, I stopped the motorcycle, raised the seat, and took out the Browning. The first sign of life heard on the pampas that morning was the sound of a bullet entering the firing chamber.

CHAPTER FIVE

Tierra del Fuego:
A Fraternal Encounter

The Land Rover had left highly visible tracks in the broom grass of the pampas. I followed them at top speed to the foot of the rising bluff. Galinsky was so sure of himself, he hadn't taken the trouble to hide his vehicle. He was even careless enough to leave the car-rental papers in the glove compartment, with his full name spelled out. I opened the hood, tore out the ignition wires, and started climbing along the edge of the ravine.

The motorcycle skidded on the slick grass, but the powerful motor kept it leaping forward. I felt like a horseman in the Seventh Cavalry, a sort of avenger, summoned to arrive on the scene just in time to avert a tragedy—a sovereign bit of stupidity, as I realized about fifty yards from the top of the hill. If I kept going on the motorcycle, the noise from the engine would alert Galinsky.

I continued the climb on foot. Large black birds were circling in a cloudless sky. A few yards from the top of the hill, I dropped into the grass and dragged myself the rest of the way up on my elbows. The tin roof shone in the early morning light. I decided to take a roundabout path down the hill, to make sure the sun stayed at my back the whole time.

When I arrived at the wooden cross stuck in a mound of earth, I discovered that I was shedding white feathers. Pedro de Valdivia's ski jacket hadn't withstood my downhill crawl. That made one more debt I owed Shorty. On the cross I read two words: Franz Stahl; and a few yards beyond I caught sight of something that compelled me to take out my automatic. There lay two dead dogs, eliminated by a good marksman. He'd blown their heads off.

All right, Belmonte, the time has come to show you're still good for something, I said to myself, running a zigzag course toward the back door of the house. I made my entrance wrapped in a cloud of dust and sparks that broke loose along with the door hinges. I dropped to the ground, looking for a head to plug with .765-caliber bullets, but all I saw was the disorder wrought by either a hurricane or a treasure hunter with no time to waste.

Slowly I stood up on my two feet. I surveyed the remains of Galinsky's search, from right to left, keeping my finger on the trigger the whole time. Then I saw the woman.

I've seen a lot of dead people. I've always noticed

something grotesque about them, as if the instant when life abandoned them arrived so suddenly, they hadn't had time to arrange their bodies in a dignified or harmonious position. The woman had been strung up by her wrists, from the mantel of a tall fireplace. Her flabby legs were bent back, so that the whole weight of her body hung from her arms, which seemed abnormally long. She was naked from the waist up. There were burn marks all over her face and torso.

I set the gun down on the mantelpiece. I cut the ropes with one hand and with my other arm supported the weight of her body. I laid her on the floor. The expression of horror on her face indicated that she had died in the throes of torture. As I was covering her with a sheet, I thought that if she had shared Hillermann's secret, she would surely have betrayed it. Galinsky was an efficient torturer. The burns were only skin deep, with no charring of the flesh, to avoid his victim's fainting. I cursed myself for not having put the motorcycle out of commission when I left it halfway up the hill. I stood up, and felt something cold press against my right ear.

"Move slowly. Very carefully," said the owner of the gun.

I let myself be prodded toward a chair.

"Sit. With your hands on your shoulders."

I obeyed. He unglued the gun barrel from my ear and, keeping it aimed at me, sat on the edge of a table.

"Who are you?" he asked.

"It doesn't matter, Frank Galinsky."

The man aiming his nine-millimeter Colt at me was a good six feet two, with blond hair, well cut, and blue eyes that couldn't help but reveal his surprise.

"Where do you know my name from?"

"You left a lot of clues. Too many. The Major will not trust you again."

"I see you know a lot. Who the hell are you?"

"My name is Juan Belmonte. We never met, till now."

"Like the famous bullfighter. Tell me about my mistakes."

"One: You should have cleaned up Moreira's place after killing him. I was there and found the key to the P.O. box. Two: You wrote him using the initials of your tag, your cover name: Werner Schroeders. It's in your file, with the German police. Three: You left the old man alive at the general store. That's a lot of gaffes for a former intelligence official. Too many for a man from Cottbus."

"We're getting old. But I assure you, with you I won't make any mistakes. I suppose you know what I'm looking for."

"Of course. It wasn't necessary to kill the woman. Like you, I came from Germany to find the Wandering Crescent Collection. But there's one big difference between us. I know where the coins are."

"Great. So we can do business. You look like a guy

who's fairly attached to his skin. What I did to the woman will be child's play compared to what I'll do to you."

"I believe you. Someone who was nothing but a repulsive red fascist all his life has no scruples. But it won't be easy for you. She knew where the coins were hidden, too. Do you realize, *Genosse?* You're just a bunch of garbage, incapable of acting without orders. Sheer garbage. That's what you are. An Ossi."

I saw him press the trigger on his Colt. The gleam in his eyes gave him away. He longed to shoot me, but his hands were tied. He wanted to kill me, but not until he found out whether I was telling the truth. I had to play for time. Mansur, Aguirre, and Ana had to be on the way.

"I'm going to count to three. Where are the coins? One."

"Do you take me for an idiot? You don't know what to believe. You won't touch a hair on my head until you've made me talk. Were you all that dumb at Cottbus? Or is it something in your diet?"

" . . . two . . ."

"Agreed. If you're going to eliminate me, you ought to know that I owe you one. I always wanted to put a couple of bullets into Moreira. We knew each other from way back. I ought to tell you the story of what he did in Nicaragua. I was there. You're talking to a guerrilla, Galinsky. I had a chance to test my courage. Besides marching tight-assed in parades, were you ever in combat?"

" . . . three . . ."

The bullet entered my left foot, at the instep. I felt the shock, nailing my foot to the floor, then the burning and right after that, the pain climbing my leg.

"I was in Angola and Mozambique. The boys in Samora Machel taught me a fair amount about this kind of game. If, as you say, you were a guerrilla, you ought to know it. You start with one foot, you follow up with the other, and little by little the lead adds up. We're going to play another round. One . . ."

The pain was creeping up my leg. Blood had begun trickling out of my shoe. I remembered the two dead dogs. A Colt like the one Galinsky wielded usually has a clip with nine bullets. He still had six left.

"Where did you learn Spanish? You speak it with a Central American accent. Do you know the expression Hey, you bastard, you screwed up? That's what just happened to you. You screwed up. Hillermann hid the coins far away from here. You'll have to carry me. Hey, you bastard, you screwed up."

" . . . two . . ."

"The Spanish language has a long list of insults and they all suit you to a T. Bastard, dope, jerk, son of a bitch, low-life, prepuce, twit, birdbrain, but the insult that suits you best comes from your own language: Ossi."

"Didn't you understand the rules of the game? Why the insults? After all, you and I are comrades. You were fighting to build socialism, and I was defending it. Three . . ."

He raised his gun and I dropped to the floor, as the report from a double-barreled shotgun shook the room. The impact from the spray of gunshot knocked Galinsky off the table. He landed at my feet, blood and guts pouring from his midsection.

Carlos Cano stood in the doorway.

"Why did you wait so long to shoot?" I complained from the ground.

"I liked the catalog of insults. Damn. He put a hole in your paw."

Aguirre, Mansur, and the mute woman came in after Cano. Trembling at the carnage, they didn't know what to do. Ana clung to Mansur's breast, holding back the heaves.

"Be strong, I'm going to take off your shoe," Aguirre said.

"I'll hold him down. This guy's got a thick hide," Cano noted.

The bullet had entered and exited cleanly. Aguirre thought the bones looked all right. He disinfected the wound and bandaged it. Then he tended to the bodies of Griselda and Galinsky.

"Cano, how did you get here?"

"I don't know. I suppose I was intrigued by the story of the treasure. When I saw you going off yesterday, I thought maybe I could lend you a hand, and I went back to Puerto Nuevo. I spent the night there. At crack of dawn, I showed up in Tres Vistas just as your friends were coming this way. We saw the dead dogs, I asked Mansur for his shotgun, and you know the rest."

"Not bad, for a dropout."

"And the coins? Do you really know where they are?"

"Damn son of a bitch, you were right outside the whole time!"

Cano shrugged his shoulders. He lit a couple of cigarettes, placed one in my mouth, and we burst out laughing. Aguirre waited patiently for us to calm down.

"I know where they are. Deliver us from that filth," he said, and gestured for us to follow him.

Outside, those ugly black birds were still circling overhead.

CHAPTER SIX

Santiago, Chile:
A Last Cup of Coffee

My legs were trembling as I went through the door of the little bar. I took the stool closest to the exit so that I could keep an eye on the street and the house across the way. I ordered coffee, and the waiter launched into a lengthy apology, ending in a hymn of praise for Nescafé. I said it didn't matter, and while I was waiting I discovered that despite the heat, the morning sunshine, the trees in full leaf, Santiago was submerged in a dull atmosphere of sadness, definitely. The city is sad. That's the title Díaz Eterovic gave the only *roman noir* set in Santiago. I read it once in Hamburg. The city is sad. Damn it, Belmonte, you have to pull yourself together, to go through with your greatest undertaking yet. Get your strength together, to walk out of here and cross the street.

All I have to do is cross the street. That's all, Verónica,

my love. Cross the street, press the black Bakelite button of the doorbell, and I'll be with you, at last I'll confront your reality of absence and silence. I'm frightened. Then let me finish a last cup of coffee in all these years apart.

From the bar, I took a long look at Señora Ana's house. The wound in my foot still hurt, but I didn't care. I stirred my coffee and reviewed events in far-off Tierra del Fuego for the last time.

Just three days ago, Aguirre had clambered onto the shiny tin roof of Hillermann's house. Cano followed him. With a hammer they loosened the nails holding the strips of tin in place, and from between the joints they removed the accursed golden coins. Ingenious German. He had even gone to the trouble of daubing them with tar, to conceal their glint.

One after another, they fell to where I was standing. With a pocketknife, I scraped away the layer of tar, and those sixty-three cold coins, as cold as the crescent moon engraved on their face, shone again with the brilliant luster human ambition had preserved through the centuries.

"Take away this filth," Aguirre said. And all that wealth lay scattered on the grass, mixed up with manure from the worn-out horses, while he, Cano, Mansur, and Ana attended respectfully to the dead.

"I suppose we have to report all this to the police," I said, gathering the coins.

"Forget it. If we alert the carabineros, word will get around, others will imagine there's more gold, and this area will be full of undesirables. Get going, and see to it that this filth is removed far from Tierra del Fuego. We know what to do with the dead," Mansur said.

"You're right. Buried treasure is only valuable as something to chat about during the long winters," Cano agreed.

I phoned Kramer from the airport in Punta Arenas.

"I have your garbage. All of it."

"Bravo, Belmonte. I knew you wouldn't fail me. Was it difficult?"

"What's the difference? Now it's up to you to carry out your part of the bargain."

"As soon as I have those objects on my desk."

I left some change on the counter and limped out of the bar. The city was still sad, although it was summer, although not a single cloud intervened between humankind and the heavens, although not a single black bird was circling overhead. And so I set out to cross the street, Verónica, my love, wondering why we're so afraid to look life in the face, we who have seen the golden glitter of death.

Hamburg 1993–Paris 1994

ALLISON & BUSBY FICTION

Simon Beckett
Fine Lines
Animals

Philip Callow
The Magnolia
The Painter's Confessions

Hella S. Haasse
Threshold of Fire
The Scarlet City

Catherine Heath
Lady on the Burning Deck
Behaving Badly

Chester Himes
Cast the First Stone
Collected Stories
The End of a Primitive
Pink Toes
Run Man Run

Tom Holland
Attis

R. C. Hutchinson
A Child Possessed
Johanna at Daybreak
Recollection of a Journey

Dan Jacobson
The Evidence of Love

Robert F. Jones
Tie My Bones to Her Back

Francis King
Act of Darkness
Ash on an old man's sleeve
The One and Only
The Widow

Colin MacInnes
Absolute Beginners
City of Spades
Mr Love and Justice
The Colin MacInnes Omnibus

Indira Mahindra
The End Play

Demetria Martinez
Mother Tongue

Susanna Mitchell
The Colour of His Hair

Bill Naughton
Alfie

Matthew Parkhill
And I Loved Them Madly

Alison Prince
The Witching Tree

Diana Pullein Thompson
Choosing

Ishmael Reed
Japanese by Spring
Reckless Eyeballing
The Terrible Threes
The Terrible Twos
The Free-Lance Pallbearers
Yellow Back Radio Broke-Down

Françoise Sagan
Engagements of the Heart
Evasion
Incidental Music
The Leash
The Unmade Bed

Budd Schulberg
The Disenchanted
The Harder They Fall
Love, Action, Laughter and
    Other Sad Stories
On the Waterfront
What Makes Sammy Run?

Debbie Taylor
The Children Who Sleep
    by the River

B. Traven
Government
The Carreta
March to the Monteriá
Trozas
The Rebellion of the Hanged

Etienne Van Heerden
Ancestral Voices
Mad Dog and Other Stories

Tom Wakefield
War Paint